# DEATHLY
# TICKET
### *to*
# SPAIN

## DONNA BASHAW

Deathly Ticket To Spain

Donna Bashaw

1st Edition

Printed in the USA

ISBN (Print Edition): 978-1-09833-024-8

ISBN (eBook Edition): 978-1-09833-025-5

*Dedicated to my forever patient husband, Phil,*
*who supports me no matter what wild idea I may have.*

# ACKNOWLEDGMENTS

I must thank those who spent hours reading and re-reading this novel as the story and mystery developed: My husband Phil, my daughter-in-law and writer of crime, Pam, and my two fellow bookclub members, Anne and Angela Jones.

## DISCLAIMER

Although the travel sites, hotels, and restaurants mentioned in this book are actual establishments, the story and all the characters in the book are simply figments of my imagination. This is a work of fiction. Any resemblance to actual events or persons, living or dead, is entirely coincidental.

# DEATHLY
# TICKET
*to*
# SPAIN

*The world is a book and those who do not travel read only one page.*

—St. Augustine

# ENVY TRAVEL

Dear Agatha and Dorothy,

I am so pleased that you have chosen Envy Travel for your trip to Spain and Portugal, and thank you for placing in us your confidence for your travel needs. I have found that it is helpful for our clients to have a list of the tour members ahead of time. You may wish to bring this list with you on your trip in case you need a reminder of the names of your fellow travelers. If you are like me, it takes a while to remember names.

Those who will be on the tour are:

**Dorothy Collins**                    Laguna Hills, Calif.
*Traveling with Agatha Johnson*

**Dave & Diane Dixon**               Troy, Ohio

**Rubio & Nancy Garcia**            Santa Barbara, Calif.
*Traveling with Ken and Lora Zimmerman*

**Agatha Johnson**                    Laguna Hills, Calif.
*Traveling with Dorothy Collins*

**Johnson Family**                    San Diego, Calif.
*Ted and Linda Johnson, and their two*
*children, Chelsie and Teddy*

**Marian Locker**                     Fullerton, Calif.

**Stanley Morgan**                    Kansas City, Kansas
*Will meet us in Europe as he has been*
*studying there for the past year*

| | |
|---|---|
| **Dan Rogers** | Los Angeles, Calif. |
| *Traveling with his brother, Rick Rogers* | |
| **Rick Rogers** | Chicago, Ill. |
| *Traveling with his brother, Dan Rogers* | |
| **Robert Thoma** | Laguna Hills, Calif. |
| **Jessica Whitley** | San Francisco, Calif. |
| **Ken & Lora Zimmerman** | Santa Barbara, Calif. |
| *Traveling with Nancy and Rubio Garcia* | |

Again, thank you for choosing Envy Travel. Your friends will truly be envious of the adventure upon which you are about to embark. I look forward to meeting you soon.

Very truly yours,

**Katie Matsen**

# CHAPTER 1

*Day 1*

---

*USA to Madrid: Pick up at your home to take you to LAX. Overnight flight to Madrid.*

---

"Dorothy, DOROTHY, for heaven's sake, hurry up! We're going to miss our flight."

Agatha Johnson looked ahead, searching for their gate number. There it is! Four gates down on the left.

Why had security been so slow? She and Dorothy couldn't miss their flight to Madrid! They just couldn't, not after all the months of planning!

Agatha glanced back to see where Dorothy was. She was even further behind than before. She looked like she was moving in slow motion.

"Dorothy, hurry," she yelled again.

Agatha's heart was pounding and her legs burned, feeling like they would give out at any moment. She heard another announcement for them over the airport speaker:

"Agatha Johnson and Dorothy Collins, please report to Gate D14. You have one minute to board your aircraft. This is the last call for passengers on Flight 142 to Chicago continuing on to Madrid."

Agatha put forth her last ounce of strength but she reached the gate just as the boarding door closed.

"No," she yelled. "No!" Agatha ran to the door and tried to open it, setting off a loud alarm.

Agatha's eyes popped open.

"Oh my gosh," she thought. "It was just a dream—actually, a nightmare." She was disoriented and the alarm from her dream was still ringing in her ears. For a moment Agatha was afraid she overslept and the nightmare might come true. Looking over at the bedside clock she was relieved to see it was five o'clock, and she realized both her bedside alarm and her cell phone alarm were ringing. She had set both of them last night in case one of them didn't go off. Throwing back her covers, she jumped out of bed and silenced them. Her heart was pounding from her dream and she had to take a minute to calm down.

Fifteen minutes later Agatha was pulling on her clothes when she heard her roommate's, Dorothy Collin's, alarm blaring *The Star-Spangled Banner* from her room down the hall. Dorothy said she used that song for her alarm because she always automatically stood up for the national anthem. It always got her right out of bed and on her feet when she heard it.

Dorothy and Agatha both stayed up well after midnight the night before packing their suitcases for the first of what they hoped would be many exciting trips abroad during their retirement years. Agatha and Dorothy each had their own bedroom with an attached bath in their new condo in Leisure World, a fifty-plus community, which allowed them to prepare for the big day without hampering each other.

Agatha and Dorothy were about to embark on the first day of their adventure. Two sets of new luggage sat by the front door, one navy blue with a colorful stripe for Agatha and one hot pink for Dorothy. They'd chosen easy-to-find colors that wouldn't get mixed up with the predominately black luggage usually seen at the airport. Just to make sure, bright red tags from the tour company with their names and telephone numbers adorned each piece.* (Reader note: at each star there is a travel tip or a delicious indigenous recipe chosen for you by Agatha and Dorothy at the end of the chapters.)

Agatha was the first to reach the kitchen after dressing quickly in her new navy pantsuit with the white sailor top. She thought it looked cute on her pleasantly rounded figure. She loved her new hairstyle, having had it layered and cut very short—easy to care for on the trip. Agatha was sixty-plus but still refused to color her hair, even though it was now naturally "highlighted" with gray. She'd been born a real red-head, and she'd always considered her thick, wavy hair her best asset. Agatha never colored her hair and she "wasn't about to start now"—a phrase she would say to Dorothy when Dorothy encouraged her to color it. Which was often!

Agatha put the kettle on to heat water for herbal tea, both Agatha's and Dorothy's beverage of choice. About fifty herbal tea bags of various kinds were tucked into a corner of each of their suitcases along with a few favorite snack items. They wouldn't starve even if they didn't like the food on the trip. They weren't particularly picky eaters, but one never knew if the food in foreign places would be to their taste. They were prepared!

"I can't believe that tonight we will be in Spain!" thought Agatha excitedly as she pulled mugs and plates from the cupboard and placed them on their small kitchen table. As happy as she and her husband Bud had been in their life together, the one thing they had not had in common was the desire to travel. Agatha's longtime best friend, Dorothy, also always wanted to travel but hadn't been able to do so because of personal responsibilities, i.e. the need to care for aging parents and a disabled brother. But now the time had come for them both, and they would soon be on their way to checking off items on their travel bucket list.

Dorothy rushed into the kitchen about twenty minutes before the van was due to take them to the airport. She looked great in her new hot pink sweat suit that matched her luggage. She had a trim figure and she kept her long hair a lovely golden blond making her look about ten years younger than her actual age, which was the same as Agatha's.

"Tea and toast are ready," said Agatha as she smiled at her friend. "That is about all we have time for. I don't know about you, but I'm too excited to eat anything else anyway."

"Me, too. Thanks for fixing it. Can you believe we're actually leaving today? We will be in Madrid in just a few hours. I don't think I slept a wink last night."

"That's why I fixed Chamomile tea, to calm us both down."

"Mmm, good!" Dorothy said as she took her first sip of tea. "Please pass the orange marmalade. Marmalade is big in Europe, you know. I can hardly wait to eat the real thing."

"This is the real thing," laughed Agatha. "It's just made here in the U.S. instead of in Europe. I'm sure they have good and bad marmalade in Europe too. This happens to be excellent orange marmalade made right here in California."

The doorbell rang, startling them both.

Agatha and Dorothy grinned at each other, and Agatha jumped up scrambling to put their dishes into the sink.

"They're a little early. You get the door and have the luggage loaded while I rinse the dishes," said Agatha.

Dorothy was already headed for the door. She would have left the dirty dishes on the table.

"Hi!" Dorothy said as she flung open the door.

"Hi!" replied a tattoo-covered young man with a big smile. "I'm Ken from Envy Tours. Are you ready to go?"

"We sure are. The luggage is right here. Agatha," Dorothy called, "let's go!"

"I'm ready," Agatha said as she hustled into the living room. "I have the checklist. Let's see—luggage, purses, carry-on with travel books, wallets, passports, money, credit and debit cards, cell phone, and medication. We've got it all. Let's go!"

After loading the luggage, Ken escorted the ladies to the van.

"Have a great trip," their neighbor, Jake Porter, called from next door. Jake, a retired police detective, was always an early riser and was in his front yard doing stretches for his morning run.

"Thanks! We will," Agatha answered, and then stopped short. "Oh, my goodness! Jake, I meant to call you last night and forgot. Could you do us a favor?"

"Sure! What do you need?"

"We have some new furniture being delivered next Monday. It was supposed to be delivered this week but didn't make it. Would you mind letting the delivery men in?"

"Of course. Be glad to."

"We already gave you our key. Let's see, the receipt is in my purse. Yes, here it is," Agatha said as she dug through her purse and pulled out a yellow piece of paper. "Just call this number Monday morning to check the delivery time. Thank you so much. I hope you don't mind doing this. We'll owe you one."

"No problem. Do you have my card with contact info if you need anything?"

"Yes, thanks!" said Agatha. "I have it with me. Here, I'll write our phone number on the back of the furniture receipt. They said the number will work in Europe. Isn't that amazing? Technology is great—often baffling—but great."

"Agatha, Ken says we need to go," called Dorothy.

"Okay, I'm coming," said Agatha.

"Bye, and again, have a good trip," said Jake giving her a hug and a big kiss on the cheek.

Agatha was surprised by the friendly kiss but pleased as she turned and hurried to the van.

"Jake is one good-looking man," thought Agatha. They'd only been neighbors a few weeks but had actually known each other for many years. Agatha was a retired criminal court clerk and Jake was in the courtroom often testifying against one bad guy or another when he had been a detective with the Santa Ana Police Department. Agatha lost track of Jake when he had been kicked upstairs in the department. She was surprised, but pleasantly so, when she and Dorothy moved into their new home and found that Jake lived in the connecting duplex. Jake told them that he hated being a paper pusher and so decided to retire early. He still did some consulting work for the department but was now doing his detecting mostly in front of a computer.

Ken assisted Dorothy and Agatha up into the vehicle. He pointed to the portly, mostly bald man sitting in the van and said, "This is Robbie. Robbie, this is Agatha and Dorothy."

"Well, well, well, hello, lovely ladies," Robbie said scooting over to make room for them.

"Good morning," said Agatha as she and Dorothy settled into their seats.

"You now begin your trip," said Ken smiling at his passengers, "of the Enviable Tour of Spain, Morocco, and Portugal. Ladies, here are your tour IDs. Just put them around your neck."

Ken handed each one of the ladies a bright red, laminated card on a black lanyard. It matched the one Robbie had around his neck, and it said Envy Tours in large black letters with the traveler's first name printed below.

"Do we have to wear these the whole trip?" asked Dorothy frowning. "It clashes with most of the clothes I brought."

"You will look lovely no matter what color combination you wear," Robbie commented as he gave Dorothy the once-over.

"Why thank you," said Dorothy with a polite smile. "I guess it will be alright."

"Do you live in Leisure World?" Dorothy asked Robbie.

"I sure do. I live just a couple of blocks over. We'll have to get together after the trip and compare pictures," Robbie said as he moved his eyebrows up and down at Dorothy in a Groucho Marx manner.

Agatha rolled her eyes, glad she wasn't sitting next to Robbie.

"To answer your question about the badges, Dorothy," said Ken, "it is helpful to wear them at all times. They assist you in finding other members of your tour if you become separated, and it has your tour leader's name and cell number on the back in case you get separated from the group."

"OK boss, we will wear them at all times," said Robbie saluting Ken and grinning at Dorothy and Agatha. "Even in the shower."

As Ken began driving, he adopted his tour guide role. "You are in for a truly enviable trip," he extolled. "You will see magnificent vistas, exotic architecture, and you will experience three very different cultures. You'll travel through Spain and Portugal and then take a trip across the Strait of Gibraltar to the world of Morocco's romantic Casbah."

"Ah, that's for me. Will you accompany me to the Casbah, beautiful lady?" Robbie said in his best Humphrey Bogart imitation to Dorothy, while putting his arm around her on the back of the seat.

Dorothy thought she could smell alcohol on Robbie's breath, and rolled her eyes at Agatha, moving a little farther away from him.

"Robbie may end up being a bit of a pain in the neck," she thought to herself.

"Anyway," Ken continued, "you'll discover wonderful Madrid with the incredible art of the Prado, and then you will travel south to Andalusia past the white windmills of Don Quixote. In the Moorish hilltop city of Granada, you'll stroll through the beautiful Alhambra. On the sun-drenched Costa del Sol, you can relax by azure waters. And, in lively Seville, you'll sip wine amidst the whirl of a Flamenco show."

"Oh boy, another highlight—booze. But do they have anything stronger than wine?" Robbie interrupted.

"I'm sure they can accommodate you with whatever you wish to drink," Ken answered continuing smoothly. "After Seville, you will pass by the beautiful Mediterranean sea coast on your way to Lisbon, Portugal. You may explore the seafaring monuments and manicured gardens of beautiful Lisbon before returning to Spain and the charming Baroque town of Salamanca. You'll stop at the ancient walled city of Segovia and then return to Madrid for a sumptuous final dinner with your fellow travelers. You are in store for a truly wonderful trip."

"It does sound like a dream trip, doesn't it Dotty?" said Agatha sighing.

"Dotty? Dotty is it? I love the name Dotty," said Robbie.

"I always say that it is better to be Dotty than dotty in your old age," he continued laughing obnoxiously at his own joke.

The girls looked at each other and rolled their eyes—again.

"Only Agatha calls me Dotty, and has since we were young girls. Everyone else calls me Dorothy. Do you understand? You are the one who sounds dotty, as in senile." Dorothy glared at Robbie. He really was becoming annoying.

Dorothy was touchy about her name. Her mother named her after Dorothy Sayers, the mystery writer. Her mother had been a mystery buff, as was Agatha's mother, who had named her after the author, Agatha Christie. Another thing the two friends had in common.

Robbie just shrugged and taking his arm down began looking out the window.

Soon the van approached the entrance to the airport.

Agatha and Dorothy began digging into their jacket pockets for some dollar bills to tip Ken. They each had made sure they had dollar bills for tips easily available in a pocket instead of a purse so they did not have to fumble. They were feeling like very sophisticated and worldly travelers.**

A lovely blond young lady in a stylish red pantsuit and a big smile approached the van as they pulled up to the curb.

"Hi!" she exclaimed as she opened the van door and charmingly gave her well-rehearsed line. "I'm Katie, your tour guide and owner of Envy Tours. Thank you so much for joining us on this adventure. You are in for an experience that all of your friends will truly envy."

Ken jumped out of the van and ran around to join Katie. "Katie, this is Robbie, Agatha, and Dorothy."

The three exited the van and greeted Katie while Ken got their luggage out of the back.

"Go to line three or four of Madrid Airlines and check in. Ken will bring your luggage in to you while I park the van," said Katie. "Say good-bye to Ken. We'll see him again when he picks us up at the end of our trip. After you're checked in, go through security. You're free until flight time. Just be sure to be at gate C14 by eight fifteen. We're not in a block of seats while flying, so our tour group will not get together for introductions until after we land in Madrid. Arrival time in Madrid is ten-twenty tomorrow morning. It's a fourteen-hour trip to Madrid from here. Try to sleep on the second leg of the flight so you can stay awake when we get to Madrid until bed-time. If you do this, it will make your jet lag easier.*** Any questions?"

The three shook their heads no and went inside the terminal. Robbie headed for line three, so Agatha and Dorothy went to line four.

"Maybe we can lose him," said Dorothy. "I hope everyone else on the tour isn't as obnoxious."

"I don't think they could be," chuckled Agatha.

Once the two friends finally made it through the long lines at security, there actually wasn't that much time before they had to be at the gate. They noticed Robbie sitting in a bar with a drink in his hand as they walked past.

"With any luck, maybe he'll drink too much and miss the flight," quipped Dorothy.

They saw a few Envy Tour red badges as the flight to Washington D.C. loaded. They all looked like nice people. Of course, looks can be deceiving. Robbie had looked nice enough at first!

"By the time we return home these people will be our friends. At least most of them will be." thought Agatha. "I can't believe this is actually happening. We've been planning this for so long."

Agatha and Dorothy spent the first leg of their flight going over travel books and practicing the few phrases of Spanish and Portuguese they thought they should know for the trip.****

On the second leg of the journey, they found themselves seated in the middle section of a jumbo jet with a very nice middle-aged couple who were also on the tour. Robbie passed them when he boarded but was deep in conversation with a beautiful dark-haired girl who also had on a red tour tag. He either didn't see Agatha and Dorothy or was no longer interested! Whew!

The attractive couple seated with Agatha and Dorothy were from a little town in Ohio and also sported red tags. Dorothy started a conversation with them as soon as they were all seated and buckled in.

"I actually don't have to 'envy' the trip you're taking since it appears that we're on the same tour," Dorothy said with a big smile. "I'm Dorothy Collins and this is my friend Agatha Johnson. Oh, excuse me, we are Dorothy and Agatha. I guess last names are not used much on this tour."

"We are Dave and Diane Dixon. Oh, excuse me, Dave and Diane," Diane said laughing, "and it is true all of our friends back home are envying us. We're from Troy, Ohio. Where are you from?"

"We're from Laguna Hills, California. We're newly retired and ready to travel," answered Agatha. "We're so excited about this trip. It's the first time out of the country for both of us."

"It's the first time out of the country for us, too," said Dave. "Actually, Diane won this trip. She got all expenses paid for two and even some spending money. Can you believe it? Otherwise there is no way we could have afforded a trip like this. I'm a fireman and Diane is a nurse."

"Wow, you won the whole trip? That's incredible," said Dotty. "How did you win it?

"Apparently it had something to do with that big national retirement organization," explained Dave. "What's it called? Something with initials. Anyway, Diane turned fifty-five this year, and the letter we got said that a few of its members win trips each year, and she had won one. Diane wasn't happy to be considered "old" since she's only fifty-six, but we were thrilled with the trip."

"That's amazing. Maybe we'll be lucky enough to win a trip sometime, Agatha."

"Maybe. I haven't heard of that contest before. You would think they would announce the winners in the AARP magazine, but I haven't seen anything like that. The organization has a lot of members, so the chance of winning would be small. Congratulations!"

Their conversation was interrupted by an announcement by the Captain.

"This is your Captain, Captain Rojas. We want to thank you for flying Madrid Airlines. The weather looks good across the Atlantic, and we expect a smooth flight. However, while seated, please keep your safety belt buckled for your safety. The estimated time of arrival is 10:20 a.m. Madrid time. The flight attendants are here to make your flight more comfortable. Drinks will be served as soon as we are in the air, followed by dinner. Following dinner, we'll be showing the movie *On the Next Tide*. We do not have a full flight, so if you wish to change your seats, you may do so once we are in the air and the safety belt sign has been turned off. Now, please sit back, relax, and enjoy your flight."

Dorothy thought she had heard a whoop out of Robbie from somewhere in the back of the plane when the Captain said they would soon be serving drinks. What an idiot he is, she mused to herself, and if he gets drunk he will be even more of a problem. Oh well, it's just part of the adventure of traveling, I guess. You meet all kinds of people.

"You said you had not been able to travel before now. Why was that?" asked Diane turning to Agatha.

"Well, I had a great husband but he had no desire to travel. He would reluctantly go along on a few trips in the States, and, of course, we would visit our three children after they were grown and moved away, but Bud was always eager to get back home to 'his chair, his books and his TV,'" said Agatha adding quotes with her fingers

"Bud always said," Agatha continued, "that he could go anywhere he wanted through books and television, without leaving the comfort of his own favorite chair. Secretly, I always suspected that he didn't like to fly, he was much more willing to go on driving trips, although he never would admit to that. I, however, want to experience everything first hand, and all over the world."

"Me too," said Diane. "We really couldn't afford to travel much before this. We are so grateful for this opportunity. How about you, Dorothy? A lot of teachers get to travel during their summers. You weren't able to do that?"

"Unfortunately, no," answered Dorothy. "I had a disabled brother who needed a lot of care. As my parents became more elderly I was needed more and more at home. I never married so I'm grateful I was able to be home to help. My little brother was greatly impaired, but he was so sweet and loving. I loved him so much. My parents and brother are all deceased now and I am free to travel with my best friend."

"Dorothy and I have known each other our whole lives, and how perfect that we can travel now—together. So much fun!" said Agatha.

Dave, Diane, Dorothy, and Agatha enjoyed chatting, and they all thought the dinner was surprisingly good for a meal on a plane. After they had eaten and the attendants had finished cleaning up after the meal, Dorothy and Agatha decided to take a walk up and down the aisles before the movie started.*****

They headed toward the back of the plane, temporarily forgetting that Robbie was back there somewhere. Suddenly he jumped up and announced way too loudly, "Dorothy, Agatha, here I am."

"As if we were looking for him," whispered Dorothy to Agatha a bit perturbed.

"Come meet this pretty little lady who is also touring with us. Jessica, meet Dorothy and Agatha."

Jessica was the raven-haired beauty they had seen with Robbie earlier. Poor thing to be seated next to Robbie. She had absolutely no expression on her face, although she kept rubbing her hands in an agitated manner as she looked up at them and merely nodded her head.

Robbie had apparently pumped some information out of her as he said she was from Northern California and was an executive with a pharmaceutical firm.

Dorothy and Agatha were finally able to extricate themselves from Robbie's blather, use the tightly quartered rest rooms, and return to their seats just in time for the movie to start. Dorothy and Agatha both enjoyed the romantic comedy immensely and, when it was over, decided one more trip to the rest room was in order before trying to go to sleep.

This time they cut across the plane to go up the other aisle to avoid Robby.

"It looks like we didn't have to sneak to the rest room after all," said Dorothy when they reached the rear of the plane. "Robbie is asleep. He probably didn't like the chic flick."

Agatha looked across the plane and could see Robbie with the side of his head leaning against the window, a blanket pulled up to his chin. His eyes were closed, but his mouth hung open with some saliva running from the corner.

"He can't keep his mouth closed even while sleeping," quipped Agatha. "Yuck!"

They saw Jessica, now on the opposite side of the plane from Robbie, in a different seat. She, too, appeared to be sleeping, though she looked pale.

"I guess Jessica escaped Robbie. She looks like she's not feeling well," said Dorothy. "I wouldn't feel well either if I had been forced to sit next to Robbie for very long. The short trip to the airport almost did me in."

"True," agreed Agatha.

Most of the passengers were settling down to try to sleep a little before landing. The lights were low, and Dorothy and Agatha decided to take a nap after returning to their seats. Diane was already asleep, and only Dave stayed awake on their row reading a travel book and taking notes about places he wanted to see and things he wanted to do on the trip.

# TRAVEL TIPS FROM AGATHA AND DOROTHY

*Put something on your luggage which makes it easy to identify for fast pick-up at baggage claim. The vast majority of luggage is black, so add a brightly-colored belt, ribbon, or tag on each piece.

**On travel day, it's helpful to carry tip money in an easy-to-get-to pocket so there is no need to fumble with wallets to then find only large bills available. Plan ahead and look like a sophisticated traveler when giving tips.

***Jet lag on an international flight is no fun and can ruin the first day or two of your trip. Here are a few things that help:

- Stay hydrated on the plane.

- Avoid alcohol and caffeine.

- Try to sleep on the plane.

- A few days before your trip, start to change your body's time clock.

- When arriving at your destination, take only a short power nap and then stay awake until bedtime.

- If necessary, take one to three milligrams of melatonin before bedtime for the first few days of your trip. This will help you sleep throughout the night.

****It's only polite to learn a few phrases in the language of the country or countries you are visiting. Agatha and Dorothy chose to learn:

|           | Spanish | Portuguese  |
|-----------|---------|-------------|
| hello     | *hola*  | *ola*       |
| good-bye  | *adios* | *adeus*     |
| thank you | *gracias* | *obrigado(a)* |

| excuse me | *perdon* | *perdao* |
| where is ??? | *donde es* | *onde es* |
| how much? | *cuanto* | *quanto* |
| do you speak English? | *hablas ingles* | fala ingles |

*****Be sure to walk around and stretch your legs on a long plane trip to avoid swollen ankles or, worse yet, blood clots. Also, there is often a card on the back of the seat in front of you with exercises you can do at your seat. Do them!

# CHAPTER 2

## Day 2

*Arrive Madrid: After your arrival in Madrid, you will be transferred to your hotel for a relaxing two-night stay. This evening, enjoy a Welcome Reception with your Tour Director.*

An hour outside Madrid, the passengers began to stir when the lights in the cabin came up and the Captain made the announcement that they would be landing in about ninety minutes.

"I guess it's time for one last trip to the rest room," said Dorothy sleepily.

As she stood up, Dave leaned over Diane and said, "The rest rooms in the rear of the plane are closed. You have to use the ones in front of us. They moved a lot of the passengers forward from the rear of the plane about an hour ago, and they won't allow anyone back there. A toilet must have overflowed or something."

"At least we can't smell it!" sniffed Agatha. "My friend was on a plane that was stuck on the tarmac for six hours last winter. The toilets were all backed up, and I guess the smell was awful."

"Yuck! Thanks for sharing," responded Dorothy. "Hey, let's wait a minute. Here comes Katie, our fearless leader."

Katie was coming up the aisle, pausing at each person wearing a red badge to give instructions. When she reached their row, she said, "We will be disembarking at Terminal 4. It's a lovely new terminal. Do not pick up your luggage. We'll take care of that. However, you may want to stop on your way out to exchange some money. The currency exchange will be on your right just after you go through customs. Follow the signs to the baggage claim area, exit out the front doors, and you will see a bright yellow bus with red lettering. Go ahead and board. I will join you as soon as we collect your luggage."

She gave them a rather weak smile and moved on.

"Well, we're not as bright and cheery after a night on the plane are we? She looked as pale as Jessica. I hope she's not sick," commented Agatha. "That could be a disaster having a sick tour guide."

"What's the matter?" Diane said groggily opening one eye.

"Nothing, but we'll be landing soon so you better try to wake up," said Dave. "Diane took a mild sleeping pill so she would sleep on the plane, and it knocked her for a loop. She hasn't moved."

"Well, she should be rested, unlike the rest of us. Come on, Agatha, let's get our hair combed and put on a little lipstick," said Dorothy as she stood up in the aisle. "I want to get back to our seats and do my first drawings in my art journal."

"Good idea. I'll make my first entry in my written journal too."*

"You're keeping journals of the trip?" asked Dave. "What a great idea!"

"Yes. Dorothy is an excellent sketch artist and will do her memories in drawings. I'm keeping a regular type of journal. You know, like a diary," said Agatha.

"I think I'll write a few comments about our trip myself," said Dave. "Diane wouldn't have much to write about so far, unless she wrote about her dreams." Dave winked at Diane.

"Very funny. I'm now awake and will join Dorothy and Agatha on the trip to the *loo*."

"Loos are in England, and this isn't even an English plane, so try going to *el inodoro*," laughed Dave as he gave Diane a big kiss on the cheek.

"I just knew 'loo' was a foreign name for a bathroom," smiled Diane.

"Loo is English. They speak English in England so I technically don't think 'loo' is a foreign word!"

"Whatever!" said Diane sticking her tongue out playfully at her husband.

An hour and fifty minutes later, Agatha and Dorothy were on the ground, through customs, and each had a wallet full of euros. They walked out into the Spanish sunshine and spotted the bright yellow bus with Envy Tours in cherry red on the side. A blond young man with tattoos on his arms was waiting beside the van.

"How did Ken beat us here?" quipped Dorothy.

"I think he's the Spanish version of Ken," said Agatha.

"I didn't know Spaniards had blond hair," commented Dorothy.

"Maybe it's bleached."

"Maybe, but he is a hunk. Hi," said Dorothy as they approached the bus, "we are Agatha and Dorothy. Are we at the right place?"

"Ah, *buenos dias*, lovely *senoritas*. My name is Jorha. Your tags tell me you are in the right place. Step into my bus, *por favor*."

Agatha and Dorothy boarded the bus. They were not the first tour members to board. Seated toward the back of the bus was a family of four—Dad snapping a picture out the window of the bus, Mom looking a bit harried after a long night on the plane with two teenagers, a girl in her late teens looking tired and bored, and a boy around thirteen with his eyes glued to some sort of game that was making annoying pinging noises.

About half way back on the other side of the bus, sat two men deep in discussion.

Agatha and Dorothy smiled at everyone and settled into the front seats. Soon a stream of tour members was boarding the bus. The Dixons boarded and sat down behind Agatha and Dorothy. Jessica came next and took a seat across from the Dixons. Next came two couples who seemed to be together, followed by a middle-aged woman with flaming red hair. Finally a young man with a huge backpack boarded. Hmm. No Robbie. Where was Robbie?

About thirty minutes later Katie finally hurried aboard the bus.

"I'm so sorry I was delayed, but I think we are ready to leave now," Katie said, flashing a small smile.

"What about Robbie?" Dorothy asked. "He hasn't come aboard yet. He was on our pickup van."

"Uhh, Robbie won't be joining us. He was taken sick on the flight."

"Oh dear! That's too bad--for him." said Dorothy. "Will he join us when he recovers?"

"Well, no. Actually--I wasn't going to tell you all this until tonight, but since you are aware that Robbie isn't with us, I'll tell you now. Regretfully Robbie Thomas, one of our tour guests, must have had a heart attack or a stroke or something on the plane. Unfortunately he passed away during the flight."

"Oh dear!" gasped Diane Dixon. "How awful for the poor man. I knew someone in Ohio by that name a long time ago."

The others on the bus made requisite comments--the usual comments people make hearing about the death of someone they didn't know under somewhat unusual circumstances.

Agatha and Dorothy felt a bit guilty about wanting to avoid poor Robbie and thinking badly of him. Poor guy! After all, he wasn't really that obnoxious, was he? Uh, yeah, he was, but he didn't deserve to die."

"Anyway," Katie continued with a forced smile, "we are going to try not to let this affect our trip. These things happen. It's part of life. I was going to have the members of our tour group introduce themselves on the bus, but we are so late I think we'll wait until tonight at the Welcome Reception. I'm sure you're all tired and eager to get to the hotel."

They all murmured their agreement as Jorha started the bus.

The trip to the hotel was uneventful. Dorothy and Agatha had their eyes glued to the window, hardly believing they were actually in Spain. Their excitement grew as they rode through the center of town. The bus soon pulled up in front of the Villa de la Reina**.

The architecture in the area was spectacular. The hotel was near the Plaza de Cibeles in the heart of Madrid and, in Agatha and Dorothy's eyes, was a most beautiful and elegant hotel.

As the weary travelers got off the bus and straggled into the hotel lobby, Jorha unloaded their luggage. A cheerful woman greeted them while a small white dog, with his tail wagging as fast as he could wag it, yapped a welcome.

Katie hurried to the check-in desk and soon had a handful of room key cards.

"I'll pass out the key cards, and you may go ahead to your rooms. Your luggage will be delivered to you. Katie's bright smile was back. "I know all of you are tired, but try not to take more than a forty-five minute power nap. Have all of you set your watches to local time? It is 1:08 p.m. here in Madrid."

Those who hadn't already done so began to change their watches.

"You may want to walk around the area. I have a list of places that are close to the hotel, along with directions. In general, the Spaniards are very friendly. They have all learned English in school and enjoy American TV. Most can speak at least a little English. On the list is the address and telephone number for the hotel. If you get lost, just jump into a cab and show the driver the address. Have fun and please be back by seven o'clock for our Welcome Reception."

Most of the travelers tiredly trudged up to their rooms. A few stopped at the bar across from the hotel desk for a quick drink before settling in. Agatha and Dorothy had already decided they were going to have a nice cup of tea*** in their room and then take a short nap before venturing out.

"This is pretty nice," Agatha said looking around as she stepped through the door to their room. "I loved the reception area downstairs too. So many book cases with books all around. You feel like you are in someone's home library."

"The hotel is very nice, and boy do those beds look welcoming," commented Dorothy, who made a beeline to the closer one.

"You go ahead and start your snooze. Maybe we should have our tea after we wake up. I'll stay awake until the luggage arrives and will set our travel clock alarm for forty-five minutes. Katie said a short nap. Then we can freshen up a bit, have our tea, and then start exploring."

"Sounds good to me, all except for the forty-five minute part. Oooh, this bed feels heavenly," said Dorothy lying down and shutting her eyes.

A very short forty-five minutes later, the alarm awoke the two and they struggled to wake up.

"I think you made a mistake and set the alarm for five minutes," said Dotty. "Can we sleep just a little longer? Please."

"No way," responded Agatha sitting up and looking more awake than Dotty. "Let's have our tea and start out on our first adventure in Spain. I can hardly wait."

"OK, OK," said Dotty sitting up and stretching. "Where are we going first?"

"I think we should go straight to El Corte Ingles****, the best department store in Spain and do some shopping."

"Sounds good to me."

They decided to walk, although it was a bit of a hike. That way they could fill themselves with the vibe of this international metropolis. Their stroll took them through the busy streets of downtown Madrid with tempting shops everywhere.

"I love all these small shops with shoes and clothing and household goods. I wish we had time to stop at each one," observed Dorothy.

"Me too," agreed Agatha, "but we better stick to our plan or we won't make it to El Corte which is supposed to be great for shopping."

"I don't speak much Spanish, but the Spanish here sounds different from what we hear at home," commented Dorothy.

"Yes, we're used to hearing Mexican Spanish. I imagine it's different from Spain's Spanish, just like Britain's English is different from American English."

Shopping was all they had hoped for at El Corte Ingles; two embroidered Spanish shawls, four pairs of shoes (including two pairs of espadrilles), and two pairs of dangly sterling silver earrings later, they were back in their rooms primping for the Welcome Reception. They wore their purchases to dinner and felt very sophisticated and worldly as they entered the dining room.

"You two look fabulous!" exclaimed Diane as she walked over to them holding the cute, little white dog they had seen earlier. Diane looked pretty good herself in a smart black cocktail dress and appeared to be the least tired of the group.

"You look fabulous, too," said Agatha. "Who's your friend?"

"This is Rolf. Isn't he the cutest thing?"

"That he is," said Dorothy as she stroked his little head.

"Would you care for some tapas****? There is quite a spread of what we would call appetizers against the wall over there," said Dave. "And let me get you two beautiful ladies a drink. What would you like? They have *vino de Jerez*, which is a sherry, *vino de la casa*, which is their house wine, sangria, which is a red wine fruit punch, or soft drinks.

"We're both teetotalers," answered Dorothy, "but ginger ale or tonic water with lime would be very nice."

"And show me the way to the tapas bar. That's my kind of bar. I'm starved." said Agatha.

The woman who had been at the check-in desk was now behind the tapas bar refilling some of the serving dishes.

"Rolf!" she exclaimed as Agatha, Dorothy, and Diane approached the bar. "You know you are not supposed to be in the dining room. I swear you are going to get us shut down."

"You speak English, American English," Diane said surprised. "I take it Rolf speaks English, too."

"Yes," laughed the woman, "he speaks the language of anyone who is nice to him, especially if they feed him. My name is Sophia. My husband is Spanish and the manager of the hotel, but I'm actually from Denver, Colorado. I came to Spain while in college, fell in love with the country, and with my husband, and stayed. Rolf is our naughty little dog who loves to be around people, and especially around people who may occasionally drop food."

"*Senorita*, here is your drink." One of the servers handed Diane a glass of Sangria.

"I guess Dave couldn't carry all of the drinks," said Diane as she reached for the glass. Just as she took the drink, Rolf jumped out of her arms and the drink spilled all over the floor. Rolf paused in his flight and quickly began licking up the Sangria.

"Rolf! No!" Sophia yelled.

"Too late," laughed Diane. "You are going to have one drunk little dog on your hands."

"It won't be the first time. Sangria is his drink of choice." Sophia couldn't help but laugh too as Rolf went scampering off.

Katie was also chuckling at the antics of the dog as she called the group to order.

"I want to officially welcome you to the Enviable Tour of Spain and Portugal," said Katie. "We didn't have an opportunity to introduce ourselves on the bus because we were delayed leaving the airport, so now, I would like to go around the room and have each one of you introduce yourself or your family and tell us where you are from and why you decided to take this tour. Let's start with—let's see—the Johnson family."

"Okay," responded Ted. "I'm Ted Johnson and this is my wife Linda, my daughter Chelsie, and my son Teddy. We're from San Diego, and we are on a family vacation. We try to visit a different country or two each summer. This year, it's Spain and Portugal, with a little Morocco thrown in."

Linda smiled at the group and just said, "Hi".

"Whoopie!" commented Chelsie.

Teddy who still had his electronic game with him, was so engrossed with it that he didn't realize he was being introduced and didn't even look up.

"Well their parents are trying to give them enrichment," whispered Dottie to Agatha, "but I'm not sure they're succeeding. I'm afraid that Teddy will not even know he's been to Spain and Portugal."

"Typical of his age I'm afraid, and the daughter does not seem to want to be here," Agatha whispered back.

"They probably would prefer to be with their friends this summer," said Dottie.

"Thanks, Ted," said Katie. "Dan and Rick, do you want to go next?"

"Sure," said Dan.

"I'm Dan Rogers and this is my brother Rick. I'm from LA and Rick is from Chicago. Neither of us is married, and we try to vacation together every few years so we can get caught up. We thought this tour looked interesting and here we are."

"Hmm! Too bad they are not about thirty years older," Dorothy whispered to Agatha.

"We're glad you're here," said Katie. "Okay, how about the Zimmermans and Garcias."

"Good evening. We are Lora and Ken Zimmerman and this is Nancy and Rubio Garcia," began Ken. "We're from Santa Barbara, where we live next door to each other in a retirement community. Rubio's ancestors come from southern Spain. Isn't that right, Rubio?"

"That's correct. On the Mediterranean Sea. We will be visiting some relatives when on the tour so we'll be playing hooky from some of the day trips. But, this is a trip of a lifetime for us."

"I can imagine, and I'm sure you're thrilled. I'm glad we can be a part of it," said Katie as her eyes scanned the room and stopped on a tall redheaded woman who looked to be in her forties. "Marian, would you like to go next?"

"Sure. I am Marian the librarian," Marian giggled. The others in the room also laughed softly. "Actually I am Marian Locker, and I am a librarian. I live in Fullerton, California, and I am a librarian at the university there. I have always wanted to see Spain and Portugal, so here I am."

"And we are happy you are with us," Katie said and then looked around the room. "Stanley, how about you?"

"I'm Stanley Morgan from Kansas City, Kansas. I'm a college student and have been in Europe this past year studying. My grandparents arranged for me to join this tour as my twenty-first birthday gift. It's the last thing I will do before returning home after being in Europe for ten months."

"When is your birthday?" asked Katie.

"It was yesterday."

"Too bad. Dan and I would have made sure you celebrated it right," called out Dan Rogers.

"We could still celebrate," said Stanley, hopefully.

"We'll see to it that you have a good time," said Rick.

"Okay, let's see, how about Jessica next," said Katie as she moved on.

"Hello. I am Jessica Whitley," Jessica said softly. "I live in Northern California. I have had a very difficult year and decided I needed to get away from it all—so here I am."

"Poor little thing," whispered Dorothy to Agatha. "I wonder if she has been through a divorce?"

"I don't know, but I imagine the men on the tour will be willing to try to cheer her up. She is really lovely," Agatha whispered back.

Katie called on the Dixons next.

"We are Diane and Dave Dixon from Troy, Ohio, and we won this trip through a contest. It happened at a great time in our lives. Our last child just went off to college and we are, I believe they call it, empty nesters. We are so excited to be here."

"Here, here," said Ken Zimmerman.

"Well, I have no idea how they selected this tour for your prize," puzzled Katie, "but I am happy they did and they paid your way in full. How lovely for you, and we are glad you are here! Maybe you will bring good luck to the tour. Anyway, last but not least, Agatha and Dorothy."

Agatha was about to open her mouth when a handsome young man burst through the door from the kitchen and said to Sophia, "Mom, come quick. I think Rolf is dead!

# TRAVEL TIPS FROM AGATHA AND DOROTHY

*Almost all tourists take pictures when they travel, but a written narrative to go with the pictures keeps memories fresh so your trip can be enjoyed over and over again throughout the years. Dorothy is an artist so she enjoys making sketches with written commentary. She says the sketches, along with Agatha's snapshots, will be the basis for future art projects.

**The Villa de la Reina is a lovely moderately priced hotel located in the heart of Madrid. It features an excellent buffet breakfast with sixty—count them—sixty homemade baked products. Mmm!

***One of Agatha and Dorothy's favorite sources of delicious herbal teas is Teavana.com. Some of their favorites are Wild Orange Blossom Herbal Tea, Strawberry Lemonade Herbal Tea, Pineapple Kona Pop Herbal Tea, Honeybush Vanilla Herbal Tea, and Sweet Fruit Garden Herbal Tea.

****Tapa means "to cover" or, as a noun, a top. Tapas started when bartenders began to put a slice of cheese or ham over the drink they were serving. No one is quite sure why they did this. However, this practice led to todays tapas which are small dishes of something edible. Common tapas dishes include meatballs (see recipe below), olives, cod, spicy sausage, prawns, thinly sliced ham, bread topped with tomato, oil, garlic and salt, etc. You get the idea.

Albondigas (meatballs in tomato sauce) was one of Agatha and Dorothy's favorite tapas. Agatha talked Sophia into giving her the recipe, which she will share with you:

### ALBONDIGAS

Ingredients:

2 tablespoons of olive oil

1 pound ground beef or 1/2 pound ground beef and 1/2 pound ground pork

1-1/2 cups fresh white bread crumbs (or more if desired or needed)

1 egg

2 tablespoons grated Manchego or Parmesan cheese

1 tablespoon tomato paste

3 cloves garlic, chopped fine

2 scallions, chopped fine

2 teaspoons chopped fresh thyme

1/2 teaspoon turmeric

Salt and pepper, to taste

2 cups (16 oz.) canned plum tomatoes, chopped

2 tablespoons red wine

2 teaspoons chopped fresh basil leaves

2 teaspoons chopped fresh rosemary

Directions:

1. In a bowl, thoroughly mix together the beef, bread crumbs, cheese, tomato paste, garlic, scallions, egg, thyme, turmeric, salt, and pepper. Using your hands, shape the mixture into 12 to 15 firm balls.

2. Heat the olive oil in a skillet over medium-high heat. Add the meatballs and cook for several minutes or until browned on all sides.

3. Add the tomatoes, wine, basil, and rosemary. Simmer gently for around 20 minutes, or until the meatballs are fully cooked. Season generously with salt and pepper and serve hot with crusty bread.

# CHAPTER 3

## Day 3

*Madrid: Our morning will be spent sightseeing in the beautiful Spanish capital as we view the Royal Palace, Puerta del Sol, and Plaza de Espana with its monument to Cervantes. Enjoy a highlight visit to the palatial Prado Museum, one of the world's greatest art galleries. See works by El Greco, Goya, Italian and Dutch masters. Your afternoon is at leisure.*

"I can't believe that sweet little dog is dead. The family is devastated." Diane was still upset about Rolf when the group was boarding the bus the next day.

"I'm sure alcohol isn't very good for dogs," sympathized Agatha as they settled into their seats.

"I feel so responsible. It was my drink."

"I don't know that alcohol is usually deadly! My dog is a real lush," said Rick. "After every party I have to hurry and clean up, otherwise Star drinks everything left in the glasses she can get to. It has never made her sick. I bet Rolf had a heart problem or something."

"Maybe," said Diane doubtfully. "Sophie did say Rolf had drunk Sangria before that night without any ill effects."

"I don't know why you were given that drink anyway, Diane. I didn't send it over," said Dave. "I know you don't like Sangria. Besides, Rolf caused the drink to spill. He jumped out of your arms."

"It was a terrible thing, but don't let it dampen your trip. Ouch! I'm sorry, no pun intended," smiled Agatha. "I think we should change the subject. We are going to have a very interesting day, and, I, for one, am excited."

"I am beyond excited," said Dorothy. "To think we will be at the Prado today. Agatha and I are going to spend all afternoon there."

"Yes, but first we are off to a royal palace, otherwise known as *Palacio Real*," said Katie as she boarded the bus, having caught the tail end of the conversation.

"Katie, before we start I want to ask you about the warm chocolate pudding we had for breakfast. It was like a dessert only it was served in a cup, but you couldn't really drink it. It was so thick that you had to eat it with a little spoon. It was very yummy," said Agatha.

"Yes, I thought you would like that, Agatha. Did everyone try it?" asked Katie.

About half the group had tried it for breakfast with rave reviews.

"It's a popular, traditional Spanish drink that is their version of hot chocolate, and you will find it everywhere. In Barcelona they usually serve it in small cups. Madrid often serves it in larger cups. It's called Xocolata. If you wish whip cream on it, ask for it *con Swiss*. Generally you dip churros in it. In Spain they are called Xurros.

"Mmmm, I love churros," said Teddy. "I liked that chocolate too. It was really good."

"They are really good. In Spain, a lot of times they do not put sugar on the Xurros as we do in the United States. I think in Mexico they usually put sugar and cinnamon on them," said Katie. "Sometimes the tourists are disappointed that they are not sweet enough here. Dipping them in the chocolate makes up for the lack of sugar."

"Do you think Sophia would give us the recipe for the Xocolata?" asked Agatha.

"Well," said Katie, "I happen to know that she has the recipe for the Xocolata and Xurros* to give to her visitors. Just ask her."

"Perfect," said Agatha.

"So, is everyone ready to go? Let's see! We seem to be missing Jessica."

"Jessica stopped at the bus earlier and said that she would not be going with us this morning," said Jorha in his charmingly accented English.

"Oh, did she say why?" asked Katie.

Jorha scrunched up his forehead to think and then said, "I don't think so."

"Okay, well let's go." Katie picked up her microphone and stood in the typical tour guide position with her back to the front of the bus and began her spiel as the bus started up smoothly and headed toward their destination.

"Our first stop this morning will be at the *Palacio Real,* or Royal Palace. The Royal Palace is still used, although not owned, by the King of Spain for state ceremonial activities. It is on the site of the Madrid Alcazar, which burned down in 1734. The Palace was begun in 1738 and took twenty-six years to complete. It has two thousand eight hundred rooms, of which we will see approximately fifty. The Palace was last used as a residence in 1931, before King Alfonso XIII and his wife Victoria Eugenie fled Spain."

"They probably hadn't seen each other since they were first married in a house with two thousand eight hundred rooms," quipped Stanley.

The group chuckled appreciatively.

Katie smiled and continued unfazed, "We will visit the Reception Room, the State Apartments, the Armory, and the Royal Pharmacy. You'll see a rococo room with a diamond clock, a porcelain salon, the royal chapel, the banquet room, where receptions for heads of state are still held, and the throne room."

"I think you will find something for everyone," Katie said. "For the ladies, there is room after room of art treasures and antiques, and for the gentleman, the Armory, which has a fine collection of weaponry. We'll end the tour with a stroll through the Campo del Moro, the palace gardens. Agatha, you and some of the others may prefer to take a tour through the Palace kitchens instead of the gardens. I will help you get the tickets for that tour if you wish to do it. Any questions?" Katie asked as the bus pulled up in front of the Palace. After a pause she said, "Hearing none, let's go. We will meet back on the bus at 10:30."

About a thousand camera clicks later, they had reassembled and were ready to board the bus. Once they were all settled in their seats, Katie asked if they had enjoyed the Palace. Every member of the tour answered enthusiastically in the affirmative. Even Teddy had put away his game and said that he thought the Armory was really cool and that he would like to spend more time there. Chelsie no longer had a bored expression, probably because she was no longer sitting next to her brother but was seated next to Stanley, who was being very attentive.

Dorothy was putting the final touches on a sketch of the facade of the Palace as Agatha looked on admiringly.

"A good beginning to the day," thought Katie. "After a rough start to this tour, people are finally beginning to enjoy themselves. That is very good!"

"We're going to drive through Puerta del Sol by way of the Plaza Mayor," Katie announced to the group. "There is very good shopping around this area. You may want to return later today to shop or even this evening for dinner, as there are also a lot of fine restaurants in the area. I'll give you a list of suggested activities and a list of outstanding restaurants you may want to try. Be sure that you have the card with the name and address of the hotel when you go out on your own so you can easily return by taxi."

"We are also going to stop briefly at Plaza de España so you can snap a picture of the Miguel de Cervantes of La Mancha fame. There is a statue of Don Quixote on his horse and his sidekick Sancho Panza on his mule. Behind them is a statue of the author, Cervantes, looking at his literary creations."

"I'm reading *Don Quixote de la Mancha* while on the trip. I highly recommend it," interrupted Marian.

"Hey, that is a really good idea. Where could we get a copy in English?" asked Lora.

"Yeah, I would like to read it, too," said Rick, "but I can download it on my iPad.

"I'll locate an English bookstore so we can get copies. How many would like a book?" asked Katie as she looked over the group. Several members of the tour raised their hands. "Okay! Tell you what, I'll pass around a sign-up sheet, and I'll locate and buy the books this afternoon. It shouldn't be difficult. Some of you may want to order an electronic version online if you have a handheld device of some sort with you."

"I prefer the real thing--a book with pages," commented Nancy.

"Hear, hear," said Marian always the faithful librarian.

"To each their own, I guess. Anyway, back to the tour," continued Katie. "From Plaza de España we will go to the Prado, staying there until 2:00 p.m. You'll have time to see only the highlights of the museum but you may choose to stay longer if you like. The bus will go back to the hotel at two for those who do not wish to stay but want to return to the hotel."

"Lunch is on your own. Lunch in Spain is the main meal of the day and is usually served between 2:00 and 4:00. Of course, in tourist areas, the serving time starts earlier. The typical Spanish *almuerzo*, or lunch, is made up of three or four courses starting with soup or salad, followed by seafood or a meat dish with vegetables. Dessert is generally a caramel custard called *flan*, ice cream, or fresh fruit. If you are staying at the Prado, there is a cafe as you enter the museum, which is actually very good. If you wish to return to the Palace, they have an elegant restaurant called the Cafe de Oriente,* which has a lavish décor and wonderful views of the palace. It is a bit pricey but worth it. You need reservations, so if you wish to eat there, let me know, and I'll make the reservations for you. If you're returning to the hotel, as you know from last night's tapas and breakfast this morning, the food is excellent."

Oh dear, thought Katie, why did I bring up last night? Diane's expression immediately changed when I mentioned last night. I guess it is time to sit down and shut up, which she did.

However, she was soon back on her feet as they approached the Plaza Mayor.

"We are now passing the Plaza Mayor. This Plaza was planned by Philip II, was built in the early 1600s by Philip III for his new capital, and was used for state events in the seventeenth and eighteenth centuries. The oldest building on the plaza is the *Casa de la Panaderia*, or the Bakers' Guild. It's located on the north side and is, unfortunately, not a bakery today, but currently serves as the main tourist office. This area has a lot of shops and restaurants."

"We'll soon be approaching the Plaza de España with its monument to Cervantes, which we talked about previously. We're only stopping for a few minutes, so take your pictures quickly and re-board the bus."

When their short visit to Cervantes was over and they were all were settled back on the bus, Katie announced their next stop as Museo del Prado, Madrid's most visited attraction.

Dorothy squeezed Agatha's hand in excitement.

"This museum has more than seven thousand paintings," Katie extolled, "and is one of the world's great museums. The Spanish are very proud of their museum, and with good cause. I'm going to give you a little background about the museum, and then Dorothy, a retired art teacher, has graciously agreed to tell you about some of the great works of art you may see in the museum."

This announcement evoked a smattering of applause from group.

"First a little background," continued Katie. "The neo-classical building which houses the museum was designed by Juan de Villanueva in 1785. The museum was opened in 1819, when Ferdinand VII transferred the royal painting collection there. Only about a thousand and five hundred works are on display at any one time, though they have many, many more works, but even at that you cannot see everything in a short visit. The museum has ongoing renovations which were started in the 1980s and continue as a permanent effort to display their incredible collection effectively. There is also a new entrance for the museum, and as you enter there is a museum shop and the cafe which I mentioned earlier. Dorothy, why don't you tell us about the art?"

"Thanks, Katie, I'd love to," said Dorothy as she took Katie's place at the front of the bus. "It's always my pleasure to share my love of art, which I did as a high school teacher for over thirty-five years."

"I bet we will be better behaved than you students," joked Rick.

"I don't know," retorted Dorothy, "I can't kick you out of class if you misbehave."

The group chuckled.

"The Prado collection was started by the royalty in Spain," said Dorothy, "and was greatly added to by the Habsburgs, especially Charles V, and by the Bourbons. The Prado, of course, has the greatest collection of Spanish paintings anywhere in the world, but there are also many paintings from the Italian High Renaissance and Flemish art. Of the Spanish artists, pay special attention to Velázques, Goya, El Greco, and Murillo."

Rubio raised his hand in the back of the bus.

"Yes, Rubio. Do you have a question?"

I have heard of Velázques, Goya, and the great El Greco, but who is Murillo?" asked Rubio.

"Ahh, yes. Since you asked, I will start with him," answered Dorothy. "Bartolome Estaban Murillo was born in 1617 and died in 1682 at the age of sixty-four."

"Young!" commented Lora Zimmerman.

"And getting younger all the time." responded Nancy Garcia.

"I would agree," said Dorothy grinning. "Anyway, he accomplished a great deal during his life. He was known primarily for his religious works, but he also painted many pictures of the woman and children whom he saw in his daily life. The Prado has about forty of his paintings, so watch for them. Does that help, Rubio?"

"Yep, thanks," responded Rubio. "I will dutifully look for his paintings. Will I get extra credit if I find all of them?"

"Of course," smiled Dorothy. "Tell you what, I will give a prize to whomever finds the most Murillo paintings. Okay? Just keep a list of the ones you find."

"Hey, that sounds fun," said Katie, "and I will even provide the prize. Go on Dorothy with the other artists"

"Okay, great. The Prado houses the most famous painting of Diego Velázquez, *Las Meninas*, or *The Maids of Honor*. It is his most well-known painting for a number of reasons. For example, artists appreciate his use of perspective and his use of lighting effects. Also, when you look at the painting, you'll notice that the queen and king are reflected in the mirror in the painting and that the artist in the foreground is Velazquez himself. The painting inspired many artists including Picasso who painted his own rendition of the work. The artist Manet said, when he saw the painting, 'After this I don't know why the rest of us paint.'"

"The Prado has the largest collection of works by Francisco de Goya, whose life spanned from 1746 to 1828," Dorothy continued. "He was the court painter for Charles IV starting in 1789. He is considered the most important Spanish artist of the late eighteenth and early nineteenth centuries. When he became deaf in 1792, his style became increasingly intense and dark. He moved to France in 1824, where he died four years later. Look for the Tapestry Paintings--*Spring, Summer, Autumn, Winter*; *The Third of May*; his *Self-Portrait*; the *Family of Charles IV*; the *Clothed Maja*; and the *Naked Maja*."

"Oh, by the way. Something interesting recently occurred at the museum. The art world was stunned when the Prado announced that two famous paintings previously thought to be painted by Goya are, in fact, not by Goya. These paintings are now described as 'attributed' to Goya and not as 'painted by' Goya. Others works may be found not to be authentic. There was such a market for Goyas at the turn of the twentieth century that art dealers kept finding "long-lost" Goyas. Now the experts have to try to distinguish the real thing from these fakes, some of which were done by very talented artists, but not by Goya."

"I'll be sure to check out the *Naked Maja*," said Rick.

"Oh my gosh, you sound just like my high school boys," laughed Dorothy. "You will see quite a few naked women today. There are a lot of paintings by Rubens at the Prado."

"How about a prize for the person who finds the most naked women in paintings?" asked Stanley.

Chelsie giggled.

"I'll get the prize for that one," said Dan.

"Just remember this is a family tour," reminded Katie glancing at Teddy who didn't appear to be paying any attention anyway.

"To continue," said Dorothy, giving the group her 'you better behave' teacher look, "the great El Greco was born in Crete in 1541 and lived most of his life in Toledo. Note that we will be in Toledo tomorrow. El Greco died in 1614. El Greco, of course, is a nickname. It means 'The Greek', referring to his ethnic origin. His real name was Domenikos Theotokopoulos."

"I'm glad he changed his name," said Lora. "That is a mouthful! So much easier to sign his paintings El Greco."

"It certainly was," said Dorothy laughing. "He is a great painter and most people think of him as being Spanish. Scholars say his work is so individual that he belongs to no conventional style of art. As you walk through the galleries of El Greco works, you will see pictures of many of the Greek saints, the Madonna, and The Holy Family. There is also the famous painting of Saint John the Baptist."

"Okay, another prize to the first person to find the El Greco painting of John the Baptist. Note down the time you find it. You are on your honor," said Katie.

By this time, most of the passengers had brought out paper and pen to write down what they should find. The competition was on.

"As to the Italian painters," continued Dorothy, "there are paintings by Raphael, Botticelli, and Correggio. Probably the most famous Italian painting here is by Titian. It is of Venus being watched by a musician, who has eyes for her and not for his music."

"Another naked maiden?" asked Stanley.

"You will have to wait and see," smiled Dorothy. "I'm not telling!"

"There are many paintings by Flemish painters, in particular Peter Paul Rubens works, of which there are quite a few at the Prado.

These include *The Garden of Love* and *The Three Graces*. Does anyone know what Rubens is known for?" asked Dorothy.

"I know," answered Dan. "Naked fat women!"

Everyone laughed while Dorothy said they were usually called voluptuous women. "Remember, rich women at that time—the late 1500s to early 1600s—had plenty to eat and did not work; therefore, it was stylish to be heavier. In contrast, poor women had little to eat, worked many long hours, and were thus thin. Rubens painted high-class women. They were voluptuous. Times change. I personally am waiting for voluptuous to be back in style."

"Yeah! Like you're so fat! I'm the one who's—uh—voluptuous." quipped Agatha.

Everyone laughed.

The bus parked as they had arrived at the Prado. All of the passengers were so enthralled by Dorothy's lecture that they hadn't realized they were at the museum already.

Dorothy looked out the window when the bus stopped and exclaimed, "Oh my gosh, we're here!"

"We sure are," said Katie. "I am passing out a small tour book as you exit which has a suggested route through the museum that you can complete in the time we have and still see the highlights. Inside the museum is an excellent shop with other tour books if you prefer. For those of you returning to the hotel with the bus, please be back here at 2:00 p.m. If you miss the bus it is easy to catch a taxi, or you can walk. It is a bit of a hike, but not too bad. Don't forget the contests. We will see who wins tomorrow on our bus trip."

They all went their various ways in the museum, but Dorothy and Agatha kept bumping into one member or another of the tour who all had questions. Dorothy wasn't perturbed by the interruptions, and Agatha noticed that she actually enjoyed answering their questions.

"I bet she was a great teacher," thought Agatha. "She still is."

It was soon two o'clock. A few members of the tour returned to the hotel by bus, but most wanted to strike out on their own. It appeared that Agatha and Dorothy were the only ones to stay at the museum and have lunch in the museum's cafe. The food wasn't half bad, and after lunch Agatha let Dorothy bask in the art by herself while Agatha wandered through the maze of halls and spent some time in the museum gift shop. She purchased a book about the history of the museum and several prints of pictures she had seen in the gallery. She would frame them when she returned home.

The Prado closed at 8:00 p.m., and Dorothy stayed every minute she could. She emerged with a sketchbook full of drawings and two bags full of purchases.

"Was it everything you imagined?" Agatha asked as they exited the museum.

"Oh yes, and more. Thank you for letting me have a full day here. You could have gone with some of the other tour members. I hope you didn't get bored or feel like you wasted part of your day," said Dorothy.

"Absolutely not. I enjoyed every minute of it. I loved seeing the art and watching the people. I also had a lovely cup of tea and a sandwich in the cafe and relaxed reading the book I purchased in the gift shop. I even took a little nap. I had a lovely day, all in all."

"Mmmm, me too," sighed Dorothy. "I could go home right now and feel satisfied. But, I'm glad we are just getting started on our tour."

"Shall we grab some dinner before we go back to the hotel? Are you too tired or are you hungry?" asked Agatha.

"Of course I'm hungry. I didn't stop for lunch, and aren't I always hungry?" laughed Dorothy. "And, I'm too excited to be tired."

"Well, I have been looking at our Madrid guidebook, and you know what I would like to do?" Agatha asked.

"Oh, oh! I know that look. What?"

"Let's go to Casa Patas**, have some tapas, and catch the 10:30 flamenco show."

"Oh my gosh! That's a great idea," exclaimed Dorothy. "Let's find a cab."

It was after midnight by the time they returned to the hotel. Katie was in the lobby and greeted them as they came through the doors.

"Did you have a good time today," Katie asked.

"We had a great time! A tremendous time! An experience of a lifetime!" exuded Dorothy.

"We did have a fabulous time," laughed Agatha. "After the Prado we ended the evening at Casa Patas and watched a terrific flamenco show. It was wonderful."

"I loved the guitar playing, the singing, and the dancing," said Dorothy. "They were all so expressive, and the costumes were beautiful."

"I loved the rhythms they kept with their feet." added Agatha. "They stomp with such power. It's got to be hard on the knees. Oh, and I loved the castanets. I would love to learn to play the castanets."

"That's wonderful," smiled Katie. "I've heard the show is really good there. How was the food?"

"Delicious," said Dorothy.

"I'm surprised you are talking about the flamenco show, Dorothy. I thought you would be all enthused about the Prado," said Katie.

"I loved, loved, loved the Prado," said Dorothy. "I spent all day in that wonderful place. Agatha was so patient and allowed me all the time I wanted. I found lots of favorite paintings, and I could gaze at them as long as I wished to. It was wonderful."

"I'm sure you enjoyed it," said Katie.

"One world-class art museum checked off my bucket list," said Dorothy yawning.

Agatha was yawning too.

"I won't keep you two up," said Katie laughing, "I know you must be really tired. Jet lag is a killer. But, I want to let you know that we will be leaving an hour later in the morning than scheduled."

"That doesn't sound all bad," said Dorothy as she noted the time on her watch. "Why are we leaving late? Do we look that tired?"

"No," chuckled Katie. "Jorha has to take the bus in to get the windshield fixed. Apparently a truck threw up a rock, and it went right through the front windshield on the way back to the hotel. I had my back to the windshield when it happened. It scared me to half to death."

"I bet! I'm glad you weren't hurt, but that's terrible! I've had a rock hit my windshield while driving before. It does scare you. Well, at least we'll have an extra hour of sleep. Sounds fine to me. Are you waiting up for everyone?" asked Agatha.

"Yes, I want everyone to be able to take advantage of the extra sleep," replied Katie.

"I'm sorry if we kept you up. Are we the last in," asked Dorothy.

"No, you are not the last. Dan and Rick are still not in."

"Well, hopefully you won't have to wait too long for them," said Agatha yawning again.

"I don't mind staying up, so long as they're having a good time. You ladies have a good night's sleep," said Katie.

"You too," replied Agatha and Dorothy.

"See you in the morning."

## *SOPHIE'S RECIPE FOR XOCOLATA:

Ingredients:

1 tablespoon cornstarch

2 tablespoon whole milk or half and half

2 cups whole milk

Scant 1/4 teaspoon fine sea salt

4-1/2 oz. dark chocolate (70 to 75%), chopped

1/4 cup unsweetened Dutch-process cocoa powder, sifted

3/4 teaspoon vanilla extract

Directions:

1. Put saucepan back on medium-low heat. Stir the cornstarch mixture and add it to the chocolate. Simmer the mixture, stirring constantly. (Scrape the bottom of the pan often with a rubber spatula to limit scorching) Simmer until chocolate is thickened and bubbly around the edges. This takes about three minutes.

2. Remove pan from heat and whisk in the vanilla.

(Optional: blend the chocolate with an immersion blender until very smooth and shiny)

Pour into small cups.

Top with whip cream and sprinkle with shaved chocolate. (Optional)

## SOPHIE'S RECIPE FOR XURROS:

Ingredients:

1 cup all-purpose flour (not self-rising)

1 teaspoon baking powder

pinch of fine sea salt

1 tablespoon olive oil

1 cup boiling water

2+ cups oil for frying

Directions:

1. Mix flour, baking powder, and salt in a bowl. Add oil and water and mix until just combined. (It should be stiff, not watery) Let set for about ten minutes and then transfer dough to piping bag - use a cookie press with a 1/3 star tip or a churro press.

2. Heat oil over medium heat. Pipe six inch lengths into hot oil. (Snip off with scissors) You can do three or four at a time. Cook two to three minutes, rolling them occasionally, until they are golden, not brown.

3. Drain on a paper towel. In the first batch try one to make sure they are done and not doughy in the middle.

In Spain they often do not roll them in sugar and/or cinnamon sugar if dipping in the chocolate. If you wish to do so, use 1/4 cup super fine sugar (caster sugar) and 2 tsp. ground cinnamon. Combine and roll the hot Xurros, after draining, in the mixture.

**Cafe de Oriente, Plaza de Oriete 2, is very elegant, with lavish decor and wonderful views of the palace.

***Casa Patas, Calle Canizares 10, is said to have the best, and most authentic, flamenco dancing in Madrid.

# CHAPTER 4

## Day 4

---

*Madrid — Toledo — Cordoba: This morning we drive to the ancient Castilian capital of Toledo. A local resident expert will lead our sightseeing tour of a thirteenth-century Gothic Cathedral, a synagogue, and Santo Tome, home to one of El Greco's most famous paintings. There will be time to shop for the famous damascened Toledo steel with its gold and silver inlay work before continuing south through the rugged landscapes of Don Quixote's La Mancha with its white windmills to the Andalusian city of Cordoba.*

---

"Good morning, everyone," said Katie as she surveyed her group of sleepy tourists. Most of them had stayed out late the night before and were very grateful for the extra hour of sleep. "I just spoke to Jorha, and he will be here in about ten minutes. Our bus has a new windshield and is ready for our trip to Toledo and Cordoba."

The group was tired but anxious to get on with their second full day of touring.

The time passed quickly as the group talked among themselves, sharing how they had spent their previous afternoon and evening, and soon their red-and-yellow bus pulled up in front of the hotel.

"All aboard," said Jorha as he entered through the front doors and began picking up luggage to load on the bus.

"*Adios*," called Sophia from the front desk. "Come back to see us soon."

The travelers called out their good-byes, but Diane went back to Sophia to again tell her how sorry she was about her little dog.

Diane was the last one to board the bus and was greeted by Agatha's rear end sticking out into the aisle as Agatha was leaning over inspecting the back of her seat.

"What are you doing, Agatha?" asked Diane.

"Agatha thinks she has found a hole in her seat made by the rock yesterday," said Dorothy.

"Yes, and I think the rock is still in there. Do either of you have a nail file that I can use to dig it out?" asked Agatha.

"I have one," said Dorothy as she began searching through her purse. "You better do it before Jorha or Katie comes. They probably would not be happy with you making a bigger hole in the seat."

"I'm not making a bigger hole. I'm just probing in the hole that is already here. Geez, it's really in there deep."

"Oh, oh! Here they come," exclaimed Diane.

"Okay, I'll wait until later," said Agatha as she seated herself. Obviously, she also thought Jorha and Katie would not appreciate her digging around in the seat. But, doggone it, she was curious about what kind of rock could go all the way through the windshield and bury itself in the seat. It would have buried itself in her if she had been sitting there. Rocks had occasionally hit her windshield while she was driving at home, but they always just pitted, or at worse, cracked the windshield, if they did anything. They never penetrated the window. Oh well, she would try again later. In the meantime she was going to enjoy another day on this fabulous tour.

As the bus started, Katie assumed her place at the front of the bus.

"Good morning again," she said brightly. "We are leaving Madrid today and traveling south to the beautiful city of Toledo. After touring Toledo, we will continue on to Cordoba, where we'll spend the night. I think you will enjoy the hotel tonight. It is actually a parador.* The Spanish governments runs state-owned inns call paradores. The government has converted deserted castles, monasteries, palaces, and other buildings into hotels. There are approximately eighty-six of them in Spain.

"Sounds like we're sharing bathrooms tonight," commented Stanley as Chelsie giggled.

"On the contrary," said Katie, the Spanish government has gone to great expense to include modern bathrooms and steam heat while maintaining classic Spanish architecture when possible. They also serve meals that are comprised of typical dishes from the region in which they are located."

"We'll be staying at Parador de Cordoba** located in a suburb of Cordoba," continued Katie. "It's on the site of a former caliphate palace. The parador itself is quite modern, but it's the grounds and the food that you will especially enjoy. There's a lovely garden, Los Naranjos, where the first palm trees planted in Europe can be found. There is also a spectacular view of the city from a large terrace. You may want to enjoy a drink there tonight. For dinner, I recommend their dining room, where they offer two unusual cold soups — *salmorejo cordobes*, or vegetable soup,*** and the *gazpacho blanco de almendra*, or almond soup****. They also serve delicious local sausages and a wonderful steak in a green sauce."

"You're making me hungry, and we just had breakfast," said Lora. "I intend to try the almond soup. That's so unusual."

"I'm sure you will enjoy your meal," said Katie. "First, however, we're going to Toledo, which is located just forty-two miles southwest of

Madrid. Toledo was the former Castilian capital until the 1500s when Madrid became the political center. It's a unique city with Roman, Visigothic, Arab, Jewish, and Christian influences. It's located in a bend in the Tagus River and stands atop a hill, making its approach very picturesque. Its skyline still looks very much like El Greco's painting, *View of Toledo*, which often hangs in New York's Metropolitan Museum of Art when it's not in Toledo. Have you seen that painting, Dorothy?"

"Actually, I believe I have. I went to the Metropolitan as a college student, so it's been awhile," smiled Dorothy.

"What's a Visigothic?" asked Rick.

"I know," said Marian.

"Good, because I'm not too sure," said Katie. "Go ahead and explain."

"The Visigoths were a Germanic tribe that defeated the Romans around 400 AD and sacked Rome. They migrated throughout Europe, and some settled in Spain and Portugal," explained Marian.

"Oh yeah! I kind of remember them. They terrorized Europe for a while, right?" asked Rick.

"That's true," responded Marian. "They were pretty brutal people."

"Hey! I think it is time to decide who won the prizes from yesterday's tour of the Prado," interrupted Stanley. "I think Chelsie and I won them all."

"No way," responded Teddy. "I bet I won the nude women contest."

"Teddy!" his mom, exclaimed.

Teddy had obviously been paying attention yesterday.

"Okay!" laughed Katie. "I have a questionnaire for you to fill out for each contest question. That way you will not know what others are saying."

"What! Do you think we would cheat?" asked Rick facetiously.

"Of course not," responded Katie rolling her eyes. "You are all on your honor. Anyway, the first prize will be for the person who found the most paintings by Murillo. You were to list the names of the ones you found."

"The next prize goes to the person who found the most naked women," reminded Dan. "I said I would win that prize."

"Bet you didn't," said Teddy.

"All right, put the number you found at the bottom of the page. I didn't actually include that one, but we can provide a booby prize."

The whole group laughed at Katie's faux pas as she blushed when she realized what she had said.

"To continue," said Katie chuckling. "Write down the time you found the El Greco painting of John the Baptist, assuming you found it. Last, write down whether or not Venus was clothed in the Titian picture. That is your bonus question."

Katie passed around the sheets of paper with pencils.

Everyone began busily filling them out.

Agatha looked across the aisle and noticed Jessica sitting by herself.

"You're probably confused by all of this since you were not with us yesterday," said Agatha.

Jessica gave her a small smile and turned her head to look out the window again, but Agatha was not going to be deterred and slid across the aisle next to her.

"Did you have a good day yesterday?" Agatha asked.

Jessica jumped when she realized Agatha was sitting right next to her.

"Yes, it was all right," said Jessica softly. "I mostly just wanted to rest. I haven't been well and wanted to get away from home to recuperate. I didn't want to travel completely alone, so I decided to join a tour."

"Have you been to Spain and Portugal before?" asked Agatha.

Jessica paused before she responded. "Yes, I have seen most of the sights on a past trip. I think I want to try to sleep now before we get to Toledo, if you don't mind."

"Of course, dear," said Agatha. "If there is anything Dorothy or I can do for you, don't hesitate to ask."

"Thank you. That's very kind of you," said Jessica and then leaned her head back and closed her eyes.

Agatha moved back to her seat.

"Talkative, huh!" whispered Dorothy.

"Not too much," murmured Agatha.

"I'll come down the aisle and collect your sheets now, if you're ready," announced Katie. "I'll announce the winners momentarily."

"What are we going to win?" asked Teddy.

"You shall see," smiled Katie. "You're assuming you are going to win something?"

"Of course," said Teddy.

A few minutes later Katie arose to announce the winners after consulting with Dorothy.

"Okay!" The first prize is for the person who found the most paintings by Murillo. The winner is—drum roll please — Marian with twenty-two. You win a ten-euro gift certificate for dinner tonight at our parador."

"Oh, that's wonderful," exclaimed Marian. "Thank you so much."

"Good job," said Dorothy. "The museum owns forty paintings but not all of them are on display at any one time. So the person who wrote down forty was obviously cheating and the whole questionnaire has been discarded. You know who you are."

The bus was silent.

"Anyway, on to the next prize," said Katie with enthusiasm. "Let's see who found El Greco's *John the Baptist* first. That was Stanley who found it in six minutes. How did you find it so fast Stanley?"

"I Googled the museum and found a site that told me where various paintings were located, and I went directly to the painting."

"Ahh, technology! Very good. You also get a ten-euro gift certificate for dinner."

"Hey! Thanks. Chelsie, will you have dinner with me tonight?" asked Stanley.

Chelsie shyly answered yes, as the rest of the group chuckled, including her parents.

"Now, for the last, uh, prize," said Katie.

"Yeah, we know, the booby prize," called out Dan.

"Well, Teddy, you were right. You won by almost double," said Katie.

"What!" exclaimed Rick. "Impossible! How did he do that?"

"Well, Teddy?" asked Katie.

"I found pictures with multiples," said Teddy.

"Multiples! What do you mean?" asked Rick.

Dorothy laughed and said, "Well, for example, he found a picture by Hieronymus Bosch called *Triptych of the Garden of Delights* which has more than one hundred nudes, and he took the time to count them. Most of the other paintings he has listed have multiples, too, although not as many as the Garden of Delights painting. Good job Teddy."

"What do I get!" asked Teddy.

"Actually, the prize is Spanish candy called *turron*," said Katie. "It's a nougat made from almonds and honey. It's particularly popular at Christmastime. You get a whole box."

"Perfect," answered Teddy. "My parents pay for my dinner anyway."

Again, laughter filled the bus, which was music to Katie's ears.

"Those of you who found the Titian picture may each take a piece of *turron* candy from my box, which I will pass around."

"Oh well, I didn't need the calories, and I still had fun finding the paintings," conceded Rick.

"Maybe we can think of some more contests," suggested Dorothy.

"That's fine with me," said Katie.

Katie sat down in her seat, and they all settled back for the balance of the trip to Toledo as Jorha turned up the Spanish music that was playing on the radio. The travelers chatted, gazed out the window, napped, or read *Don Quixote* or travel books as they road through the beautiful countryside. Of course Teddy was still busy with his electronic game. However, he was no longer so annoying to the other passengers, as Stanley had shown him how to turn off the pinging noise.

What seemed like a very short time later, Katie stood up again and said, "We're about three miles from Toledo, and you can soon begin to see the skyline in the distance. It's really quite spectacular."

"Wow, it is so beautiful," said Agatha a little later as they crossed the Tagus River.

"To think that this is where El Greco lived and worked," said Dorothy. "I'm so excited."

They soon pulled into a large parking area where several other buses were parked.

"We will disembark here," said Katie, "and ride up the escalator to the old city. It's a short walk then to the central square, Plaza de

Zocodover, where we will start our walking tour of the city which will include a visit to the *Cathedral de Toledo* built between 1227 and 1493. Its beautiful alter piece tells the story of the entire New Testament. Also, there are stunning stained glass windows and pictures by El Greco, Velázquez, and Goya throughout. After the walking tour there will be about an hour and a half of free time for shopping before we start our journey to Cordoba. Be sure to eat lunch or grab something to eat on the bus. If you want a leisurely lunch, you might want to try a favorite Toledan dish, *perdiz estofada a la toledana*, which is partridge stew with white wine, bay leaf, and onions. Very tasty!"

"Better than a partridge in a pear tree," quipped Dan. "A bird in the hand, or in the tummy, and all that."

"Much better," chuckled Katie. "During the free time, I believe Dorothy and Agatha are going to Casa-Museo del Greco, which is in the old Jewish quarter. The museum has paintings by Greco including his famous *View of Toledo* when the painting is in town, which I believe it is right now. Dorothy and Agatha said they would be happy to have anyone join them. The Zimmermans and Garcias are meeting up with some relatives of Rubio's who live here. The rest of you are free to shop, sightsee, or eat. There is a forty-minute train tour available which leaves from the main square. It offers great picture taking opportunities that you would not otherwise have. Everyone should meet the bus back here at two. Just ask a local for directions back to the main square if you have wandered afar and are having difficulty finding you way back."

"What are good things to shop for in Toledo?" inquired Lora.

"Good question," said Katie. "Toledo is known for its swords and *damasquinado*, or damascene work."

"I want to buy a sword," called out Teddy as he looked up from his game.

"Mmm! He does actually listen," commented Agatha softly to Dorothy. "We'll have to remember that."

"Oh yes! Kids his age are very good at multitasking," said Dorothy.

"These are real soldiers' swords and are quite expensive," Katie said to Teddy, and then continued, "Damascene is a Moorish art of inlaying gold, silver, or copper threads against a black matte steel backdrop. Damascene jewelry is a popular purchase and you can even see it being made in several of the jewelry stores."

"That's something I might buy," said Chelsie.

"You should try some of their marzipan, Teddy," continued Katie, "which is a specialty and is often prepared by local nuns. It's very yummy. The province of Toledo is also renowned for its pottery. They have beautiful tiles, which are easy to carry home with you, but if you decide you must have some of the larger pieces of the pottery, the shop will ship it home for you. I have a list of reputable shops and good restaurants available for you. And, oh, by the way, if you get hot while walking around, you may want to try an ice-cold creamy *horchata*\* drink. It's a drink made with tiger nuts and is a specialty of Spain. The Toledo Cafe Bar in the Plaza de Zocodover is a good spot to relax and enjoy a *horchata*, and it is right across the street from one of the best marzipan shops in town. In any event, you should have a fun morning."

"We'll be met by Maria, who will be our local guide and will take us through the cathedral and on the walking tour," Katie said, as she looked out the bus's side window. "Yup, there she is."

Jorha opened the bus doors, and Maria bounced aboard.

Maria was a tall, dark-haired beauty who was full of energy.

"*Buenos dias!*" she called out.

"*Buenos dias,*" everyone responded.

"Welcome to our beautiful city of Toledo," said Maria. "Toledo is known as the Imperial City because it was the site of the court of Charles V, the Holy Roman Emperor. It is also called the City of the Three Cultures, as we have a rich history of Christians, Muslims, and

Jews, all of whom inhabited the city during its long history. As you tour Toledo you will see the lovely sites the three cultures have created in our city.

We will take the escalator up to the old city, into the main square, and then we are going to visit our beautiful cathedral built between 1226 and 1483. It is called a Gothic masterpiece but it also features several different architectural types.

You may want to visit the Alcazar during you free time which was built originally in the tenth century. During the Muslim era, it was a fortress but was later altered a great deal by the Christians. It was all but destroyed during the Spanish Civil War when it was subject to a seventy-day siege and was rebuilt in the 1930s. It now houses an Army Museum, one of the finest in the world.

As you drove toward our city, the cathedral and the Alcazar stood out on the horizon. The look of the city as you approach has not changed much over the centuries. You come now in automobiles and busses, but it looks much as it did when it was commonly approached by foot or on horses. It still looks as it did when El Greco painted it. A print of his painting, *A View of Toledo*, is a popular souvenir. Hanging the print next to your own snap shot is a wonderful way to remember your day in Toledo.

"So, let us visit my city, Toledo. Please follow me. I am sure you will marvel at its loveliness. The cathedral is so very beautiful and ornate it will—how do you say—blow up your mind."

Everyone laughed as they exited the bus.

They all had a most enjoyable and interesting visit. The group was turned loose around noon, and individual members went their various ways.

Agatha and Dorothy really enjoyed the cathedral and then dashed to the old Jewish quarter where the *Casa Museo del Greco* housed some superb paintings by Greco. They had a little time to grab some decorative tiles, damascene jewelry, and some lunch they intended to eat on the bus.

They actually got back to the bus a little bit early in spite of their rush because Dorothy's feet were killing her since she had worn her new espadrilles instead of her walking shoes.

"You are back a little early, *Senoritas*," said Jorha as they approached.

"Sore feet," responded Dorothy. "Could you get my small suitcase out so I can change my shoes? These are not quite broken in as yet."

"No problem," said Jorha as he opened the bus doors. "*Senorita* Agatha, why don't you go ahead and board the bus and get out of the heat. The motor is on, so the air conditioning could cool down the bus."

"Works for me," said Agatha, as she quickly boarded the bus. Jorha and Dorothy went to the side of the bus to get Dorothy's suitcase.

"Hmm. This is a good chance to retrieve the rock," thought Agatha, as she put her packages in the overhead compartment and placed Dorothy's lunch on her seat.

Agatha had purchased a pair of tweezers while out shopping so she quickly inserted them in the hole, grasped the rock, and pulled it out. She was just going to take a closer look at it when the bus doors swung open again and the Zimmermans and Garcias boarded followed closely by Dorothy. Agatha stuck the rock in her pocket to look at later.

"Boy, my feet feel much better," said Dorothy as she fell into her seat. "Let's eat. I'm starved."

"Me, too!" laughed Agatha. "Let's get through the sandwiches so we can get to the marzipan."

"Good plan, or we could eat the marzipan first," suggested Dorothy.

"Hmm, not a bad idea. Say, wasn't today the day they were delivering our new furniture at home?" asked Agatha.

"Home? What home? I'm a world traveler. The world is my home," said Dorothy as Agatha rolled her eyes. "Just kidding. You're right. It was today. We should give Jake a call tonight to see if everything arrived okay."

"Good idea. It would be nice to talk to Jake anyway."

"Right," said Dorothy with a wink and a smile.

"What?" exclaimed Agatha.

"Nothing!"

The two-hundred-mile trip down to Cordoba was rather restful. They only stopped momentarily for a "potty break" and to take a quick picture by a lovely white windmill to prove they had been to Don Quixote country.

The sun was low on the horizon as they arrived at the Parador de Cordoba. The parador looked rather modern and welcoming from the exterior. They were soon all settled comfortably in their rooms.

"I really like our room," Dorothy said as she plopped down on the couch and looked around.

"Me, too," agreed Agatha. "Do you feel like taking a walk around the grounds? It's too early to call Jake, he'll still be in bed, and Katie said the grounds are beautiful."

"Sounds good to me. My feet are somewhat rested after the bus ride. Let's go!"

Dorothy and Agatha first went to the parador's restaurant and made reservations for dinner for seven that evening. Then they strolled through the gardens and the *Los Naranjos* (the orange trees), then by the courtyard with the swimming pool. Several members of the tour were already in the pool, including Chelsie, Teddy, Stanley, and the Dixons.

"Come on in. The water's great," called Dave, as he saw the ladies walk up to the edge of the pool.

"We probably should wait until we have our suits on," responded Agatha with a smile.

"You could try skinny dipping," said Stanley, as he swam up to the edge of the pool and grinned up at them.

"At our age, that certainly would clear the pool out pronto," joked Agatha.

"Speak for yourself," laughed Dorothy. "I personally have the body of a twenty-year- old."

"Really! Where are you hiding it?" asked Agatha as she rolled her eyes.

"Watch out or you will land in the pool—fully dressed," laughed Dorothy.

"I think it is time to head back to the room before we get into trouble," said Agatha.

"Works for me! Bye, everyone," said Dorothy.

As soon as the two traveling companions reached their room, Agatha sat down on the edge of the bed and dialed Jake, while Dorothy went into the bathroom to start getting ready for dinner.

"Hi, Jake," said Agatha when Jake had answered his phone.

"Hey, Agatha Ann. How's the trip going?"

"We are having a great time. We love Spain. Dorothy can't get over the fact that she has been to the Prado. It was so wonderful. Seeing world famous pictures in person is a lot different than seeing them in a book. The colors are so much more vibrant. We'll tell you all about it when we get home—probably until you are sick of hearing about it. I just thought I'd call to see if our furniture arrived today," said Agatha.

"Yup, it arrived, and it's all in place just as you directed. It looks really good."

"I'm excited to see it, assuming we eventually get home again."

"And you wouldn't eventually get home because . . ."

"Just kidding. We will get home, but we've just had a series of crazy little happenings which seem to keep delaying us."

"Really! Like what?" asked Jake.

"Well, first of all, we had one of our tour members die on the plane coming over. He had a heart attack or something."

"Geez! That's terrible. Poor guy! A trip of a lifetime and he dies before he can even get started. Too bad he couldn't have waited until he was on his way home. But at least you didn't know him yet. It probably would have been harder on you and the other tour members if he had died on the way home."

"Maybe! We did meet him on the way to the airport. He was in our pickup van and we actually thought he was kind of obnoxious. It was a bit of a relief he wasn't going to be on the tour with us." Following a pregnant silence Agatha said, "Oh, I didn't mean that the way it sounded. That was terrible. The poor guy!"

"I know you didn't mean anything," laughed Jake.

"Anyway, he died so there was a delay at the airport. Then later that day this cute little dog at the hotel died after drinking a spilt drink of sangria."

"I didn't know dogs died of alcohol intake, at least ingesting a limited amount."

"I don't think they do normally. The poor little dog must have had a heart condition or something because he didn't really drink that much. One small glass. His owner said he had lapped up spilt sangria before without it hurting him."

"And how did a dog's dying delay your trip? Did you have to wait for its funeral?" asked Jake.

"No, silly, that didn't delay us, but the next day a rock hit the windshield of the bus and broke it. We were delayed because it had to be fixed before we left the next morning. The rock embedded itself right in the back of my seat. Luckily, Dorothy and I had stayed at the Prado for the afternoon, so my seat was empty. In fact, I pulled out the rock today and stuck it in my pocket. I wanted to see what kind of rock could do that much damage. It's such a small rock. Let's see I have it right here. I was going to look more closely at it tonight. Let's see! Here it is?

"Oh my gosh!" exclaimed Agatha as she looked at the object in her hand.

"What?" asked Jake.

"This isn't a rock at all. This is a bullet!"

# TRAVEL TIPS FROM AGATHA AND DOROTHY

*Paradores are hostelries operated by the Spanish government, many of which are converted castles, palaces, and monasteries. They have the amenities of a luxury hotel but retain the historic character of the old building. Meals are served, usually including regional dishes. Advance reservations are strongly recommended. Every tourist to Spain should stay at least one night in a parador, although they do tend to be a bit expensive. Agatha and Dorothy think they are well worth it.

**Paradore de Coroba is an exception to the rule of paradores and is not a converted historical building, but it is one of the nicest paradores in Spain. It is built on the site of a former caliphate palace. The gardens are lovely and contain the first palm tree planted in Europe. The rooms are spacious, and the restaurant is excellent. Av. de la Arruzafa 33, 14012 Cordoba, 95-727-59-00.

Agatha is good at talking chefs out of some of their recipes. Here are a few she and Dorothy want to try at home.

***SALMOREJO CORDOBES (Creamy Cold Tomato Soup)

**SALMOREGO CORDOBES**

Ingredients:

2 eggs

2 ounces Serrano ham (may substitute prosciutto)

1 large clove garlic

2 pounds ripe tomatoes

8 ounces extra virgin olive oil

2 ounces red wine vinegar

Salt to taste

Directions:

1. Hard boil the eggs. Place in ice cold water to cool. Refrigerate until ready to serve.

2. Cut off hard crust from baguette, then cut into slices approximately one-half-inch thick. Pour about a one quarter inch of water into a large glass baking dish. Add bread slices and allow bread to soak for 30 minutes. Squeeze excess water out of bread slices and place in a blender or food processor.

3. Peel and mince garlic and place in food processor. Peel tomatoes and remove seeds. Add to the food processor and pour in the vinegar. Process.

4. While processing, slowly pour in oil. Continue to process until smooth. If mixture is too thick, add in a bit of cold water. Refrigerate until ready to serve.

When ready to serve, dice the Serrano ham. Peel and quarter the hard-boiled eggs. Pour the soup into four bowls. Sprinkle ham over the soup. Add two egg quarters to each bowl.

****Blanco de Almendras* (Almond Soup)

## BLANCO DE ALMENDRAS

### Chilled Almond Soup

Ingredients:

7 ounces unblanched almonds (never ready-blanched)

7 fluid ounces Spanish olive oil

3 cloves garlic, peeled

1 dessert spoon sherry vinegar

2 level teaspoons salt, or more, to taste

4 ounces black grapes, deseeded and halved

1 dessert apple, peeled, cored, and thinly sliced

Ice cubes

Directions:

1. To blanch almonds, place them in a heatproof bowl, pour in enough boiling water to cover, and leave them aside for 3 to 4 minutes. Drain and squeeze the nuts out of their skins into a bowl.

2. Put the almonds into a blender and pour in the olive oil. (The oil should just cover the almonds. If it doesn't, add a little more.) Add garlic, vinegar, and salt, and process until everything is smooth. With the motor still running, slowly add about 12 fluid ounces of cold water.

3. Pour the soup into a large bowl. If it is too thick, add a little more water. Cover the bowl and keep well chilled until you're ready to serve. Just before serving, stir in the ice cubes and ladle the soup into the chilled bowls. Garnish with the grapes and apple slices.

**Hot Almond Soup**

Ingredients:

3 tablespoons extra-virgin olive oil

1/2 cup blanched almonds (3 ounces)

2 cups 1/2-inch bread cubes

2 tablespoons chopped fresh flat-leaf parsley

2 large garlic cloves, finely chopped

1/4 teaspoon coarsely crumbled saffron threads

2 cups chicken broth

2 cups water

1/2 teaspoon salt, or to taste

1 teaspoon sherry vinegar, or to taste (optional)

Directions:

1. Heat oil in a 10-inch heavy skillet over moderately high heat until hot but not smoking. Sauté almonds in the oil, stirring constantly, until golden, about 4 minutes. Transfer almonds with a slotted spoon into the blender. Add bread cubes, parsley, garlic, and saffron to the oil in the skillet and cook over moderate heat, stirring constantly, until golden, about 2 minutes. Transfer about one-fourth of the crouton mixture to a small bowl for garnish, and then transfer the remainder to the blender. Add the broth to the blender, and puree the mixture until smooth.

2. Transfer the puree to a two- to three-quart heavy saucepan and stir in water. Simmer, uncovered, stirring occasionally, until slightly thickened, about 5 minutes. Stir in salt and vinegar and serve the soup topped with croutons.

*****Horchata-This is a popular drink made in Spain with tiger nuts, water, and sugar. Other countries use different ingredients for a similar drink also call horchata. Tiger nuts are not available in the United States, but when they returned home Dorothy found a recipe using almonds which, she says, tastes almost as good.

### HORCHATA

Ingredients:

1 pound almonds

1/2 to 1 pound sugar as desired

1 lemon

1 cinnamon stick

Directions:

1. Remove the skins from the almonds. Use the method in the recipe above or buy them already skinless. Crush or pulverize the almonds into a coarse powder.

2. In a large bowl, put 2.5 liters of water with a pinch of salt.

3. Slice and add the lemon.

4. Mix the almond powder (or mush if you blanched the almonds yourself). Cover the bowl and let sit at room temperature for two hours.

5. Add the sugar and a cinnamon stick. Stir until sugar is completely dissolved. Strain the liquid through a fine cloth. (Strain at least twice)

Keep the drink in your fridge for up to five days. Agatha likes to put it in the freezer until it is an icy slush. Mmmm good.

# CHAPTER 5

## Day 5

---

*Cordoba-Granada: Córdoba is situated in the fertile valley of the River Guadalquivir and has many architectural monuments built by the Romans, the Moors, and the early Christians. We begin our sightseeing by visiting the Mezquita-Catedral de Córdoba, famous for its candy-striped pillars, and then the magnificent eighth-century Mosque of the Caliphs, known for its eight hundred and fifty pillars of porphyry, marble, and jasper. Then we travel through the Andalusian olive groves on our way to the Moorish Granada with its spectacular views of the surrounding Sierra Nevada. In the evening, you will enjoy a Highlight Dinner of local specialties.*

---

Dorothy had been asleep when Agatha returned to their room the night before. When Agatha had realized that the "rock" was actually a bullet, she immediately contacted Katie, who called the local police. Agatha, Katie, and Jorha had all been questioned last night. The thought was that it was a stray bullet, but the bus hadn't been in a gang area when it occurred, and the Madrid police indicated that they had not had any other occurrences of expressway shootings, as occasionally happens. Where the bullet had come from was a mystery. Agatha was particularly upset since she could have been sitting in the seat in which the bullet had imbedded itself. Scary stuff!

Katie had asked Agatha not to tell any of the other tour members what she had found for now, except Dorothy of course. Agatha had already told Dorothy that the "rock" turned out to be a bullet. Not a secret Agatha could have kept from Dorothy.

Agatha was still quietly explaining what had happened the night before to Dorothy while they were at breakfast.

"Dotty, this whole trip has been one odd happening after another. Judge Smith would always say there are no true coincidences. And, I think that is true. What in the world is going on?" asked Agatha.

"That's basically what Jake said too on the phone last night, that there are no coincidences," responded Dorothy worriedly. "I was thinking, most people aren't as inquisitive as you are and probably would not have dug that bullet out of the seat. Even if someone had, they probably would not have known it was a bullet. It was kind of squashed. It didn't really look like a bullet."

"Yes. I've marked a lot of bullets into evidence in my day as a court clerk. A lot of them no longer looked like bullets. You know, I've been thinking. Do you believe someone is trying to undermine Katie's business?" said Agatha as she drank the last of her tea.

"Hmm! Now that's a possibility. Do you think…" but Dorothy was interrupted by the Dixons coming up to their table.

"We missed you last night," said Diane smiling at them. "We didn't see you in the dining room."

"Uh, well, we fell asleep after our walk and didn't wake up in time to go down to eat. We ended up just having a tray in our room," responded Agatha, thinking quickly.

"Oh! That's too bad. The food was terrific. And the view is spectacular at night from the terrace," said Dave.

"I'm sorry we missed it," said Dorothy truthfully. She was terrible at telling lies, even little white lies, so she was glad that Agatha had spoken up.

About then Katie walked into the breakfast room and announced that the bus would be leaving in about fifteen minutes. Katie looked tired and had dark circles under her eyes. All of these quirky happenings were beginning to take their toll on her.

Agatha tried to look perky and rested to the others, but she too was tired and worried. What in the world was going on? She would try to talk to Katie sometime today and ask her if she knew anyone who would wish her ill, or if there was a competitor who might be trying to harm her business. But Robbie's death and the little dog's death didn't really fit that scenario. How could someone have planned both events. Why would anyone? And to shoot a gun into a bus—seriously! No one could do that—no one would do that—not just to eliminate a competitor. Would they? Katie's tours were small. They wouldn't encroach too much into someone's business. No, none of it made sense. Coincidences after all?

All of the passengers were settled in their usual seats as Katie announced their day's agenda.

"We are starting our day at the Mezquita, Córdoba's eighth-century mosque. For Spanish Muslims, Córdoba was an important pilgrimage, second only to Mecca and Jerusalem. You'll love walking through the labyrinth of red-and-white striped arches. The Mezquita is one of the world's greatest work of Islamic architecture. But, you'll be surprised to see a sixteenth-century cathedral right in the middle of the mosque. The cathedral was built in 1523 as part of Charles V's scheme for "Christianizing" Moorish places, but when Charles learned what had been done in his name, he was not happy about it and said, "To build something ordinary, you have destroyed something unique in the world." One of the most interesting features is the *mihrab*, a shrine that once housed the Koran. So we have Islam, Christianity, and Jewish religions represented. This mosque is quite ecumenical."

"After exploring the mosque," Katie continued, "stroll through the Courtyard of the Orange Trees and look at the beautiful fountain. I would also recommend that you walk over to the fourteenth-century *Calahorra* Tower which is part of a twelfth-century fortress. The tower was built to guard the Roman Bridge of Córdoba. It is a lovely walk, and there are wonderful photo ops from the tower. Continuing in the spirit of our contests, there will be a prize for anyone climbing the sixteenth-century tower. Take a picture of the *Mezquita* from the top for proof that you were there. We will board the bus in two hours. We will then go to the Moorish Versailles, also known as the Caliph's Pleasure Palace."

"Hmm, that sounds interesting," commented Rick.

"But, it sounds 'R' rated," responded Linda.

"It's not 'R' rated any longer," said Katie. "It was constructed in the tenth century by the first caliph of *Al-Andalus, Abd ar-Rahmān* III. It was named after his favorite concubine of the harem, who was called "the brilliant.""

"Hmm, I wonder what she was brilliant at?" said Dan.

"Which should be phrased, 'I wonder at what she was brilliant,'" corrected Marian. "You wouldn't want to end a sentence with something dangling, especially in front of the children."

"Very funny," said Dan.

"Back to our agenda today," broke in Katie. "The Pleasure Palace at one time had three hundred baths and four hundred houses. After its heyday, however, the site was plundered for building materials. The royal house has been reconstructed, but most of the rest has been left in ruins. You must imagine its former majesty."

"Wow, it was a real harem," said Stanley. "It's hard to imagine that any guy could be that lucky."

"I don't know about that. I have enough trouble with one wife. I can't imagine trying to manage fifty," said Rubio as his wife poked him.

"Most of them were not wives but concubines," said Dorothy, "and they were managed often by the Sultan's mother, called the *valide* sultan, and by the eunuchs who served them.

"What's a eunuch?" asked Teddy. "Is it like a unicorn?"

"Sort of. I'll tell you later," said his Dad as everyone laughed.

"Anyway," continued Katie, "we will then have a leisurely drive through the Andalusian olive groves to tonight's destination which …" here, Katie paused to give her words some additional drama— Granada, of Arabian Night's fame."

Everyone oohed and aahed appreciatively.

"It's so beautiful! I can hardly wait for you to see it," said Katie. "Tonight's dinner, just as a reminder, is included in the tour and is a highlight, with many delicious local specialties. We should all have a wonderful day. One you will remember for many years with pleasure."

And, it was a great day. And, as it turned out, one which no one would ever forget, but not with pleasure.

The mosque was enjoyable with its beautiful arches. There was only one little hitch. Teddy did not show up at the bus on time, and his mom and dad had to go looking for him. They quickly found him sitting on a bench in the gardens, playing his electronic game, so the group wasn't delayed too long. So, all in all, so far so good.

The bus was meandering down the road at sunset when the tired tourists spotted Granada in all its glory right there in front of them.

"There it is," cried Marian. "I'm reading about Granada in the *Tales of the Alhambra*, and here we are. I'm so excited to be here."

"Oh, oh! Another book to read? I haven't finished *Don Quixote* yet. That thing is really long," complained Dave.

"Oh, but *Tales of the Alhambra* is sooo romantic," responded Marian.

"Ooo, that sounds good to me. I love a good romance novel. Who wrote it?" asked Diane.

"Washington Irving," answered Marian.

"Does the book have anyone who is headless or sleeps a lot?" asked Teddy, looking up. "I studied Washington Irving at school. *The Legend of Sleepy Hollow* is one of my favorite books."

"Good for you, and good for your teacher," exclaimed Marian. "But no, there are no headless people in this one, and no one who sleeps an exceptionally long time either."

"There, I just bought it on my iPad," said Dan.

"Okay, if I ever get through Cervantes, I'll try Irving," conceded Dave.

"Anyway," continued Katie, "Granada is located in the foothills of the Sierra Nevada. It was a stronghold for Moorish Spain. The famous Alhambra was the palace-fortress of the Nasrid Sultans. The Nasrid Dynasty was the last Muslim dynasty in the Iberian Peninsula. This fortress was built during the thirteenth and fourteenth centuries around an existing Moorish eleventh- century fortress. It consists of the *Alcazaba*, which is the old fort, the *Palacios Nazaries*, the palace, and the *Palacio de Generalife*, the summer palace, and beautiful gardens everywhere. Next door is the sixteenth-century palace of Charles V, which is in Renaissance style. Granada was the last Moorish stronghold to fall to the Christians in 1492."

"Wow! The same year Columbus sailed the ocean blue," joked Rich.

"That is true," replied Katie. "We will see the *Puerta de Elvira*, which is the gate through which Ferdinand and Isabella made their triumphant entry into Granada that year. However, it no longer has rotting heads of executed criminals hanging from its portals, as it once did."

"Shoot!" exclaimed Teddy.

"TEDDY!" exclaimed his mother as everyone laughed. "Shame on you!"

"Tonight will be a night of nights," continued Katie unfazed as usual. "Tonight we are staying at the most famous parador in Spain, the *Parador de Granada.** It's actually on the grounds of the Alhambra. The building was once part of the palace and mosque built between 1332 and 1354 that was converted in the fifteenth century to a convent. We'll also have dinner at the parador. For your dining pleasure, you will be served *gazpacho andaluz*, a cold soup of the region, *pollo a la alpujarreño*, a garlic chicken dish, and *piononos de Santa Fé* for dessert, which is cake.* There will also be a flamenco show after dinner which I'm sure you will enjoy. The dancers dance to stylized guitar music, castanets, and the hand clapping of the other dancers and often the audience. The rhythm they can keep with their feet is truly amazing. Agatha and Dorothy, did you enjoy the flamenco show you went to in Madrid?"

"Oh yes," they enthusiastically agreed. "You will all love it."

"There will also be general dancing throughout the evening," continued Katie, "to an excellent live group of instrumentalists and vocalists. Oh, and be sure to bring a wrap with you to dinner as you may want to stroll the lovely grounds after eating. It's sometimes a little cool this time of year."

"It sounds wonderful," said Diane. "What time do we eat?"

"Be in the dining room at 7:00," replied Katie.

"Are we going to the Gypsy caves tonight?" asked Stanley.

"No, and I wouldn't recommend them, although the caves themselves are interesting enough," said Katie.

"What are the Gypsy caves?" asked Rubio. "Gypsies are dangerous, aren't they?"

"At one time, thousands of Gypsies lived on the "Holy Mountain," so named for the Christians martyred there. However, in 1962 the caves were heavily damaged by rain, forcing many out of the caves, leaving only the Gypsies who were involved with tourism. And, the caves are very much a tourist trap. At night there is entertainment with guitars and castanets called the *zambra*, but anyone with any talent ends up at the more expensive clubs in town, not in the caves. The Gypsies are continually after your money, and they are very good at getting it," explained Katie.

"Well, you can't get blood out of a turnip, as they say, so maybe I'll go," said Stanley. "You game, Chelsie?"

"Sure! It sounds exciting," replied Chelsie.

"Not so fast! We need to talk about this," said her Dad. "She'll let you know tonight, Stanley."

The hotel was as wonderful as Katie had said, and all was well as the group gathered for dinner after a day of touring.

"What a beautiful shawl," said Marian as she admired Diane's new, brightly colored Spanish shawl with long black fringe.

"Thank you. I bought it in Córdoba. I thought I could wear it at home. There are so many wonderful things to buy. It's always so hard to decide," said Diane.

"Yeah, so she just buys them all," joked Dave.

"I know what you mean," said Ken. "When we get to the cruise, we will probably sink the ship with all the purchases Lora and Nancy have made."

"Boy, you can sure say that again," agreed Rubio, as their wives both gave their husbands "the look."

"Anyway," said Katie, "we have four tables by the dance floor."

"That's only enough for sixteen," commented Dorothy. "Are we missing some of our group?"

"Stanley talked us into letting Chelsie go to the Gypsy caves, and Teddy talked Stanley into taking him, too," said Ted. "It is kind of nice to have a night out alone with my wife," he added as he squeezed Linda's hand.

"Yeah, just you and Linda—and the other fourteen of us," joked Rick.

"But you are all adults," smiled Linda. "That counts for a lot."

"There are place cards with names at the seats. Of course, you can change seats if you like," said Katie.

As everyone moved into the dining room, Katie whispered to Agatha that she had put her and Dorothy at her own table with Jorha so they could talk about what was going on, and she hoped she didn't mind.

Of course Agatha didn't mind at all. She wanted to talk to Katie, too.

Most everyone seemed happy with their seating arrangements. Ken, Nancy, Lora, and Rubio were at one table. Linda, Ted, Diane, and Dave were at another. Katie had seated the two single men, Dan and Rick, with the two single women, Marian and Jessica. Yes, Jessica had actually joined the group for dinner. It's hard to pass up a free meal, especially one of this caliber.

They were all enjoying their gazpacho when Katie brought up the subject of the weird experiences they had been having on the tour.

"The Madrid police think the bullet was a result of a random shooting. I'm sure it was. I don't know what else it would be," said Katie.

"It's just such an unusual thing to have happen," said Agatha. "Not to mention scary that I could have been in that seat, or it could have easily hit you."

"I know," said Katie. "Very scary!"

"We have never had a tour member die on a tour before," said Jorha. "It is unusual to even have someone injured."

"I'm sure that's true," joined in Dorothy. "But someone did die on the tour, and, of course, there was Rolf's death also."

"Who?" asked Jorha.

"You know," responded Katie, "Sophia's dog."

"Oh, *si*! At the hotel."

"Rolf drank the spilt drink," said Agatha. "The drink was intended for Diane. I wonder if Diane would have been sick had she drunk the Sangria."

"I doubt it," said Katie. "I drank a fair amount of the Sangria myself that night without any consequences. Or, at least, without any unusual consequences."

"No one else seems to think anything too unusual is happening on this tour," said Dorothy. "We're all having a really good time. A trip we'll all remember. Oh, and our friends back home will be envious of our enviable tour," she laughed.

"Thank you, Dorothy," Katie laughed too. "I'm glad all of you are enjoying yourselves, but remember, the others don't know about the bullet, and no one had met Robbie, except for you two and Jessica, before he died. His death probably didn't really seem to have much to do with the tour. Agatha, why did you ask me if I knew anyone who would not want my business to be successful?"

"Well, when I first discovered the rock was a bullet, I was thinking maybe someone didn't want your competition. But the first two incidents don't really fit that scenario," said Agatha.

"I do such small tours, no one really cares. There are so many tour groups. Most tour companies do larger groups. I wanted to do smaller, hands-on tours. For just a little extra in the cost, I believe we give you a lot more in services and higher quality of lodgings and food."

"That's true, dear," said Dorothy. "Agatha and I chose to pay a little extra for our first time out on our own, and I'm glad we did. The reviews we read about your company were all so glowing, and we are loving this tour."

"Thank you so much," said Katie. "That means a lot to me. And that's even though you know about the bullet."

"Yes, we even know about the bullet." smiled Agatha. "Jorha, do you dance? How about taking me on a spin around the dance floor while we wait for our main dish."

"I believe that was an invitation to dance. I would be delighted, *señorita*," said Jorha as he jumped to his feet. "You do the *salsa? No?*"

"If it's a dance, I can do it. You lead, and I'll follow," said Agatha.

Several others of the tour members were already on the dance floor, and the evening proceeded most enjoyably.

The table with the singles seemed to be having an especially good time, although Jessica left right after dessert. The other three were having plenty to drink, especially Marian. She kept either Dan or Rick on the dance floor almost the whole evening.

"Marian is having a good time," commented Dorothy.

"She certainly is. I think she would like to land either Dan or Rick by the time this tour is over," said Agatha. "She sits right in front of them on the bus and spends most of her time turned backwards in her seat, talking to them."

"Yeah! They seem to like her but certainly aren't leading her on romantically. I think they are just interested in being a friend," said Dorothy.

"Mmmm," murmured Katie. She, of course, couldn't gossip about the tour members.

About then the flamenco show began. For an hour there was much clapping of hands and stamping of feet as the dancers twirled and whirled around the dance floor. When it was over they were given a standing ovation.

"Oh my," said Agatha. "That was so good. I believe it was even better than the troupe we saw in Madrid. That was so much fun. I wish I were younger and could learn to do that."

"That was really good, and now I'm thirsty. Jorha, could you see if they have some herb tea?" asked Dorothy. "I don't know how to ask for it. We want herbal and not green or black tea."

"*Si*, lovely lady, I will do so for you," said Jorha as he caught the attention of the waiter.

"Let's all have some," said Katie. "It will be lovely with the cake."

"Not for me, *gracias*," frowned Jorha, "I'll stick with the wine, but I will order for the three of you."

About then they heard a crash coming from the singles table.

"Oh, look what I did," squealed Marian. "I tipped the table and knocked our dishes onto the floor. I'm so sorry! I don't seem to be standing too well," she giggled swaying slightly.

Several waiters rushed to the rescue, assuring Marian that it was no problem.

Marian did not look too steady on her feet and reached out to Rick to steady herself.

"Maybe we should take a walk out in the fresh air," suggested Rick.

"Oh, good idea," said Marian loudly, giggling again. "But, I forgot to bring a wrap."

Diane was at the next table and heard everything Marian was saying. But then so did everyone else in the restaurant.

"Marian!" Diane said as she leaned toward her table, "Would you like to borrow my shawl? Dave and I decided to go right back to the room and not take a walk."

"I don't blame you for going right back to your room with the kids out for the evening," laughed Dan.

Diane blushed, but handed her shawl to Marian.

"Thang you," slurred Marian putting it around her. "I will take goot care of it and return it, return it—give it back to you tomorrow."

"Tomorrow, tomorrow," Marian began singing the song from the musical Orphan Annie.

"No problem," said Diane as she sat back down to finish her dessert, smiling at her husband and rolling her eyes.

"Let's go, my two big handsome men," said Marian, as she took each of them by the arm and walked them out of the room.

"Boy, it will be a lot more quiet with them gone," said Agatha.

"I'm glad she's having a nice time," said Dorothy.

Agatha and Dorothy had a great time at the dinner and returned to their room about midnight after a stroll around the grounds.

"Wow! That was so much fun," said Dorothy.

"It really was. I love to dance," said Agatha.

"I know you do. It appears that I do too, and didn't even know it," laughed Dorothy.

"Yeah, you were doing a wild salsa with Jorha."

"I wouldn't talk. You were doing a wild salsa all night with everyone. And that tango. Where did you learn to tango?"

"Bud and I loved to dance and actually took ballroom dance lessons. We even competed in dance competitions a few times. We learned a lot of different dances."

"Really," exclaimed Dorothy. "I had no idea."

"Maybe we could take some lessons when we get home."

"Together? I'm not sure I want to tango with you."

"No, silly, we would take from male teachers. They would dance with us. The only problem is the lessons are expensive, and it's really expensive if you want to compete."

"Oh, I would never compete," said Dorothy. "You do it in front of other people, don't you?"

"Yes, but you might be surprised at yourself. It's a lot of fun. Anyway, we can consider it when we get home. I didn't realize how much I missed dancing."

"Let's get to bed," suggested Dorothy. "I've missed sleeping! It's nice we get to sleep in a little tomorrow."

"Yes," agreed Agatha, "I have some shut-eye I need to catch up on."

They were soon both sound asleep, expecting a good eight hours of snooze time, but at 3:00 a.m. the phone in their room began to ring shrilly.

"Hello," said Agatha sleepily, picking up the phone beside her bed.

"Agatha, this is Katie. I'm so sorry to wake you, but you were the first one I thought of to call. Oh, Agatha, they just found Marian face down in the fountain. She's dead!"

# TRAVEL TIPS FROM AGATHA AND DOROTHY

*Paradore de Granda* is probably the most famous parador in Spain. It is located within the grounds of the Alhambra in what was a fifteenth-century convent. It's booked way in advance, so reserve early. It is also quite pricey, but Agatha and Dorothy think it's worth a splurge. Agatha and Dorothy prefer the older section, decorated with antiques. Real de la Alhambra s/n, 18,009 Granada.

**Piononos de Santa Fe* cake is a cake inspired by a pope and endorsed by kings. This small, round cake is made of custard, sponge cake, and cinnamon. Agatha couldn't talk the chef out of his recipe.

# CHAPTER 6

## Day 6

*Granada—Costa del Sol: This morning, a highlight visit to the famed Alhambra; to pass through its gates is to enter an Arabian Night's dream! A wonderland of "lace in stone," surrounded by arabesque gardens and fountains, the Alhambra affords superb views of the Old Quarter and Sacromonte, a mountain occupied by Gypsy cave dwellers. Then, we travel south to the vibrant Costa del Sol for a leisurely three-night stay. On the way, we visit a working rural olive mill for olive oil tasting. We will also join locals at the village square for an Andalusian home hosted lunch.*

Katie called a meeting for 9:30 a.m. for the tour group. Only half the group was there. Missing were the Johnson family, Stanley, Dan and Rick, and, of course, Marian. Katie was dressed in sweats that had no doubt been pulled on hastily when she was called in the middle of the night. She had very dark circles under her eyes and her usually beautiful blond hair was falling out of a pony tail.

"I'm so sorry," Katie began, "to deliver some very bad news to you this morning. Last night Marian apparently tripped and fell into the patio fountain, bumping her head, and…and then drowning in the water."

"Oh no!" exclaimed Diane.

"Marian!" murmured Jessica as she turned and looked at Diane startled.

"What!" said Rubio. "That can't be. That just can't be."

Everyone looked stunned, except for Agatha and Dorothy, who already knew the dreadful news.

"It happened sometime after dinner. Chelsie, Stanley, and Teddy found her when they were returning from the Gypsy caves. They're with the police again this morning, and, of course, Ted and Linda are with their children. Since Dan and Rick left the dinner with Marian, they too are with the police right now."

"It's believed to have been an accident," continued Katie, "but it will delay our leaving for the coast today. However, this morning will go as planned since we are staying local. The police will want to ask each of you some questions, but that will not be until late this afternoon. This morning, you can tour the Alhambra and then meet back at the hotel at noon. Then, Jorha will drive you to the town where lunch was planned and on to the tour of the olive oil vineyard for the olive oil tasting. Then, however, you will be returning to Granada instead of driving on to Costa del Sol. The good news is that we will all be staying at this lovely hotel another night. The police tell us that we should then be free to travel to the coast tomorrow morning. Any questions about today's itinerary?"

"Was Marian still dressed for the evening when they found her, or had she gone to bed and then gotten back up?" asked Ken.

"I'm sorry, everyone! I can't answer any questions about Marian right now. Police orders. Only questions about today."

"I wonder if she had my shawl with her," murmured Diane.

Katie looked at her and said, "That I can probably tell you. The shawl was floating on the water. That's what attracted Chelsie's attention. She initially thought it was you."

"Poor Chelsie," said Diane. "And poor Teddy, and Stanley too for that matter. It's horrible for anyone to find a dead body. All of them will probably have nightmares for a long time."

"That's so true," agreed Linda. "Those kids will never be the same. Some innocence has been lost forever. So awful!"

Everyone just sat there. Jessica was so pale she looked like she might faint at any minute, and Diane had tears in her eyes.

Finally, Linda said, "Isn't this the second death on this tour? What is going on?"

"It's just a fluke, I think, Linda," said Agatha quickly. "I'm sure the rest of the trip will go off without anymore crazy happenings. Horrible accidents happen, but they are rare. We all know Marian was drinking a great deal last night."

"Yes, that is true," said Rubin.

"Well, I think we should all go have a look at the Alhambra. Marian was so excited about it. She would want us to go, I'm sure," said Dorothy.

"Right. Then we will have lunch and go olive oil tasting," said Agatha. "I've heard of wine tasting, but not olive oil tasting."

"You'll enjoy it," said Katie. "There are actually many different flavors of olive oil. They add herbs and citrus to the oil, too, which is wonderful. You taste the oils on delicious crusty bread. Be sure to buy a few bottles to enjoy at home. They ship."

"Okay," continued Katie. "Go see the Alhambra and then return to the hotel. Jorha will be leaving at 12:30 for lunch. Here are your tickets for this morning."*

As the group broke up, Agatha asked Dorothy if they could return to their room before walking around the Alhambra.

"Of course," responded Dorothy. "Do you need to use the bathroom?"

"No, well maybe, but I want to call Jake. I wonder if he would do a little investigating for us. What time would it be at home?"

"Let's see, it's 8:45 a.m. right now, so it would be 5:45 in the afternoon at home," calculated Dorothy.**

"Perfect! Let's go see if he's home."

Agatha explained to Dorothy why she wanted to call Jake as they returned to their room to make the phone call.

"I'm glad we are staying another night here. This hotel is so nice," said Dorothy.

"Me, too," agreed Agatha as she placed the call to Jake. "Of course, not under these circumstances."

"Oh, of course not!" agreed Dorothy,

Jake answered on the second ring.

"Hi! This is Jake."

"Hi, Jake. This is Agatha and Dorothy. You're on speaker."

"Hey, hi! How's the trip going? Everything okay?" asked Jake cheerfully.

"The trip itself is great, but we were wondering if you would do us a favor?"

"Sure. Be glad to," responded Jake.

"You better wait until you hear what it is.

"Okay! I reserve my agreement," Jake chuckled.

"We had another 'incident' last night, this time a serious one," said Agatha.

"What kind of incident?" asked Jake, turning serious.

"One of the ladies on the tour had a bit too much to drink and apparently fell into the fountain in the patio of the hotel," explained Agatha.

"That doesn't sound too unusual after a night of partying."

"Perhaps not, but she supposedly bumped her head when she fell into the pool and she drowned."

"She died?" exclaimed Jake.

"Yes, she died," said Agatha.

Jake was silent for a moment and then said, "What do you want me to do?"

"Well, she left the party with two brothers on the tour, Dan and Rick Rogers. Could you just see if there is any connection between Marian Locker, a librarian at Cal State Fullerton and the brothers, Dan Rogers from Los Angeles and Rick Rogers from Chicago?"

"Why? Are you suspicious that this wasn't an accident?" asked Jake.

"I don't know. I hate to think it wasn't. It's just that so many odd things have happened on this trip."

"Are you not having a good time?"

"Oh, we're having a great time, or we were. The tour is wonderful, the people are wonderful. It's just that I'm getting a feeling that something fishy is going on, but, on the other hand, I don't see how all of these crazy happenings could be connected."

"What do you think, Dorothy?" asked Jake.

"I don't know," Dorothy responded slowly. "But I do know that Agatha has good instincts so I think it's worth looking into."

"Okay. I'll do a little snooping on the Internet. Are you going to be in your room so I can call you back? asked Jake.

"No," said Agatha. "We're just leaving to tour the Alhambra, then we're going to lunch, and then on to an olive oil tasting."

"The tour is just continuing on like nothing happened?"

"Well, not exactly. We were supposed to go to Costa del Sol tonight, but we are staying in Granada for another day instead while the police investigate. If they are satisfied, we go on to the coast tomorrow."

"So, do you want to call me back?"

"Yeah! I think that would be easiest, don't you Dorothy?"

"Definitely," said Dorothy.

"Okay, I'll talk to you ladies later. Just don't call me in the middle of the night. Any time after 6:00 a.m. my time is okay. Bye," said Jake.

"Bye, and thanks, Jake," said Agatha. "We owe you."

"No problem. Glad to help. Have a good day."

"All right," said Agatha as she hung up the phone. "Let's go explore the Alhambra."

"I'm game. Let's go."

Agatha and Dorothy's tour began with the *Mexuar*, also known as *Palacio Nazaries*. It's the first of the trio of palaces at the Alhambra. They especially loved the view from the Catholic chapel, which had been converted from the Hall of the Mexuar in the 1600s, and from the *Patio del Mexuar*, constructed in 1365. The Patio was where the sultan sat on large cushions to listen to petitions from his subjects, and it was richly decorated with beautiful tiles. Dorothy drew such a cute sketch in her journal of a fat sultan sitting on an even fatter pillow, which they giggled over. The *Mexuar* was built around two courtyards, one with a narrow reflecting pool flanked by myrtle trees. So lovely! And, the Court of the Lions—very impressive with a large fountain resting on twelve marble lions. This was the heart of the palace and the most private section, where the sultan enjoyed his harem. The ladies peeked into the Hall of the Two Sisters, where the sultan kept his favorite lady of the moment and shivered as they thought of living here at the beck and call of the sultan.

Agatha and Dorothy visited the infamous *Sala de los Abencerrajes*, the home of a noble family, many of whom were the rivals of the twenty-second and last emir, Boabdil. Boabdil rid himself of the problem by inviting his rivals to a banquet, where his guards entered during the meal and massacred the guests. Hmm, and we think our politics are nasty. Of course, not all meals were as risky as the Hall of the Kings, the great banquet hall of the Alhambra, was the site of many parties, orgies, and feasts. They didn't usually end in death but just in a lot of bad headaches. Pretty decadent!

When Agatha and Dorothy viewed the Court of the Window Grille, they felt sad because they were reminded of Marian and how much she would have enjoyed today. Washington Irving had lived in furnished rooms in this area when he began to write *Tales of the Alhambra*. It's just all so lovely. Marian would have loved it.

"This visit is for you, Marian," Dorothy said, giving a mock toast.

They next strolled over to the Emperor Charles V's Palace, which was built in the early 1600s. Charles paid for the palace by levying a heavy tax on the conquered Muslims. It was beautiful but, to Agatha and Dorothy, appeared very much out of place in this Moorish stronghold.

The two took a quick trip through the *Museo de la Alhambra* but skipped climbing the Watchtower at the *Alcazaba*. Too tired. They ended their morning tour with a stroll through the Generalife, the summer palace of the sultans. It had provided a retreat from the splendors of the Alhambra for each sultan and his entourage. The Generalife is known for its beautiful courtyards and gardens. Dorothy particularly liked the Oriental garden, *Patio de la Acequia*, with its long pool with water jets shooting arches above the pool. In English it's known as the Court of the Water Channel. Much less romantic-sounding. Dorothy took the time to make a sketch while Agatha took pictures and rested her tired feet. Agatha thought about putting her hot feet in the water but thought better of it.

It was soon time to return to the hotel, and they emerged from the magical world of sultans and harems. Why did that world seem so romantic when in reality it must have been pretty terrible, especially for the women. All would admit, however, it was beautiful.

Not many of the tour members showed up for the bus trip to lunch. The Zimmermans and Garcias were off visiting more of Rubio's relatives, so there were only five waiting for Jorha to bring the bus in front of the parador for loading. Agatha was surprised that Jessica had decided to go on the day trip. Also going were the Dixons.

"All aboard for lunch," called out Jorha as he opened the bus doors. "I guess there will be only six of us for lunch."

"All the more food for us," responded Dave. "I'm starved."

"Me, too," said Dorothy.

The mood lightened as they rode through the beautiful Andalusia. The *Pueblos Blancos,* or white towns, dotted the sides of the steep mountains. This area was part of the Sierra de Grazalema Natural Park. Spectacular!

They were on their way to Ronda, a little town in the Serranía de Ronda. It is one of the oldest towns in Spain. Everyone in the bus gasped as they saw the gorge spanned by a Roman stone bridge, the Puente San Miguel, over the Guadelevin River. Houses clung to the side of the mountain, looking like they could so easily fall into the five hundred-foot chasm, yet they had been there for many, many decades. The town was divided by the gorge, the older Moorish and aristocratic section on one side and the post- Reconquista section on the other.

Lunch was held in a typical Andalusian home with delicious home-style food and freshly squeezed orange juice which seemed to be available in every eating establishment in Spain.\*\*\* Because it was cool in the mountains, the tour members enjoyed the hot soup that was served. After lunch they lingered on the terrace of the home, admiring the view. Dorothy was making a sketch of the beautiful white town while Agatha was in the kitchen with the owner of the home, getting the recipe for the soup and tomato toast. Linda sat chatting quietly with Jessica while Dave wandered the grounds taking pictures. It was so peaceful, so restorative.

"I wish the whole tour could have been here," thought Agatha. "The whole tour, including Marian and Robbie."

It was soon time to leave for the ancient olive grove. Jorha was quite good at keeping his passengers entertained with stories about Christian slaves and the great bullfighting family from the area, the Romeros. He spoke especially about his boyhood hero, Pedro Romero, who killed five thousand six hundred bulls in his thirty-year career, and who was Goya's inspiration for his *Tauromaquia* series of bullfighting scenes. Where was PETA when the bulls needed them? Jorha also said that there was a cave in the area with prehistoric paintings on the walls, but that there would not be time to stop.

After a few hours of walking, tasting the wonderful olive oils, and shopping, Jorha brought the little group back to Granada. Returning there reminded them again that the last twenty-four hours had majorly changed the tour. Marian was gone.

"It's almost 9 a.m. at home," said Agatha as she and Dorothy walked to their room. "Jake said we could call him anytime after 6 a.m. his time. I'm eager to talk with him to see if he was able to learn anything about Dan, Rick, and Marian."

"Yes, but I can't believe that Dan or Rick did anything wrong," commented Dorothy.

"We'll see. The jury is out!"

Once the girls were settled in their room, Agatha put through the call.

"Hi, Jake!" said Agatha.

"Hey! How was your day?" responded Jake.

"Under the circumstances, it was really quite nice," said Agatha. "The *Pueblos Blancos* were so lovely, the lunch was yummy good, and the olive oil tasting was interesting and tasty."

"Hmmm! Olive oil instead of wine tasting. I would have to think about that one."

"Wait until you taste the oil. We shipped four different oils home. The variety available is amazing. Anyway, what did you find out about Dan, Rick, and Marian?"

"Well, I could not connect Marian with Dan or Rick prior to this trip, and I did not find out anything about Marian that was out of the ordinary. She is—was a librarian at the University in Fullerton, just as she said. However, I did find out something interesting."

"Good, and what was that?" asked Agatha.

"I found Dan Rogers in Los Angeles but no Rick Rogers in Chicago. Also, Dan Rogers does not have a brother. Therefore, there is one thing we know for sure—Dan and Rick are lying!"

# TRAVEL TIPS FROM AGATHA AND DOROTHY

*A limited number of tourists are allowed to visit the Alhambra each day. Arrive as early as possible to get tickets for the same day. To avoid the long lines, contact Banca Bilbao & Vizcaya (BBVA). Visit in person, or call 90-244-12-21, or visit the website www.alhambra-patronato.es. You will pay a $1.30 surcharge, which is worth it when saving limited vacation time.

**Agatha bought a watch with two faces before her trip. She set one face for home and one set for Spain so she always knew what time it was at home. There are also apps for your phone and iPads that will allow you to see what time it is at home.

***Almost every eating establishment has a large machine that squeezes oranges; therefore, fresh orange juice is always readily available and is very refreshing in the hot Spanish sun, and it is generally inexpensive.

# CHAPTER 7

*Day 7*

---

*This morning we will travel to Costa del Sol with the rest of the day to relax by the blue waters of the Mediterranean.*

---

It was a pretty somber group that boarded the bus in the morning. All were present - except Marian, of course. As they got started, Teddy just sat staring out the window, not even interested in his game. Chelsie sat with her mother. Her eyes were still red-rimmed from crying and from a sleepless night. Stanley sat alone with a grim look on his face.

What a shame it was the youngest members of the group who found the body, thought Agatha. It's an experience that will always be a part of them.

Agatha had seen many young people pass through the court system, some as victims, and some as witnesses. They all had that "deer in the headlights" look, just as Teddy, Chelsie, and Stanley had this morning.

Agatha's attention then shifted to Dan and Rick. Why were they lying about being brothers, she wondered. They were the last ones to see Marian alive, as far as anyone knew. But why would they hurt Marian? They seemed to all get along well, and Jake could not find any prior connection between Marian and the two men. Marian was pretty drunk last night. Maybe she did accidentally fall and hit her head. But, two people have died on this tour, as well as a little dog, and a bullet was fired through the front window of the bus. How strange all of this is!"

Dave was dozing in the seat behind Agatha and Dorothy, and Diane was sitting with Jessica. They were quietly talking, and Diane was holding Jessica's hand.

"I'm glad Diane is getting through to Jessica," whispered Agatha to Dorothy. "I tried but was unsuccessful."

"Yes, with all of this terrible stuff happening, she needs someone," said Dorothy.

Dorothy leaned forward and asked Katie how she was doing.

"Oh, I'm fine," Katie answered as she looked at Dorothy with tired eyes. "I just don't understand why this tour is under such a black cloud. It's a good group of people. Everyone gets along well, and there is no one who is really obnoxious, as often happens."

"The person who would have been obnoxious on the tour is no longer with us," said Dorothy. "Sorry, I know I shouldn't speak ill of the dead, but Robbie would have been the obnoxious one. Trust me when I say that. Seriously though, this is a great tour. We're having a wonderful time except for these, these, incidences. We're just so sad for Marian, and Robbie too, of course."

"They say lightning never strikes twice in the same place, but this time it sure did," Katie lamented.

"I'll bet the rest of the trip will be smooth sailing."

"I certainly hope so. I can't think what else could happen."

"Well, this is a beautiful drive today."

"Yes, but short. It is only sixty-four miles to Torremolinos. It'll take us about an hour and forty minutes to get there."

Sure enough, in about an hour and a half of peaceful driving, Katie was on her feet and speaking to the group.

"We have just arrived in the city of Torremolinos, one of the most famous beach resorts in Spain. We'll be staying at the Hotel Cervantes*. It's located in a shopping center and is only a seven-minute walk to the beach. It's also very close to many boutiques and open-air cafes. All of your rooms have balconies with sea views. I think you'll enjoy our accommodations. Please just have a relaxing day. Tomorrow we go to Morocco."

"Is that safe?" asked Linda. "That's part of Africa, right?"

"Oh yes! It is part of Africa, and it's perfectly safe," answered Katie. "I've been there many times."

Linda still looked a little nervous.

Upon arriving at the hotel, the tour members all headed to their rooms.

Agatha and Dorothy liked their room and immediately went out onto the balcony.

"Look at the Mediterranean Sea. Isn't it beautiful," exclaimed Dorothy.

"It certainly is. What do you want to do today?" Agatha asked.

"Shopping is always good," said Dorothy.

"True," responded Agatha. "How about we first call Jake to see what he has found out about our other tour members, then we shop till we drop, followed by a good meal and a stroll on the beach?"

"Sounds good to me," said Dorothy. "But, I just want to enjoy this view for a while. You go ahead and call Jake."

"Okay!"

Agatha went into their room and settled down in a comfy chair with a pen and pad and dialed Jake.

It rang several times before Jake picked up.

"Hi, Agatha Ann," said Jake.

"Hi, yourself," said Agatha. "We're in Torremolinos sitting in our hotel room, which has a beautiful view of the Mediterranean."

"Ahhh! Way to make a guy feel bad," quipped Jake.

"Sorry," laughed Agatha. "I didn't mean that. Well, maybe I did."

"I'm glad you're having a good time. Is the trip everything you dreamed of?"

"Yes, and more, except, of course, for the weird happenings plaguing the tour. Did you find out anything interesting about our fellow passengers?"

"I ran all the names and found a few interesting tidbits but nothing earthshaking."

"And ..."

"Let's see, I've already told you that Dan and Rick are not brothers. It appears that they both live in West Hollywood, together. Rick had his last name changed to Rogers two years ago."

"Okay, so they're probably gay. Why hide it in this day and age?"

"Who knows? The Zimmermans and Garcias are not only neighbors but also business partners. They own a frozen yogurt franchising business called Zoogies."

"Yeah, I've had Zoogies frozen yogurt. It's quite good. Very creamy."

"I also don't see that Rubio Garcia has relatives in Spain. His background is from Argentina, so what they're doing when they leave the tour to visit 'relatives' is a bit suspect.

"Hmmm. Interesting."

"Katie, your tour guide, has owned her own travel business for about five years. She was struggling until the past year or two but seems to be doing fairly well now."

"I looked at Robbie Thomas also. He has a record. Mostly petty stuff, nothing really serious."

"Have they done an autopsy on him to see why he died?" asked Agatha.

"No, his body isn't even back in the States as yet. Lots of red tape. They'll do an autopsy when he gets here. Anyway, that's about it. Everyone else checks out with the information you've given me."

"You didn't find any connections between any of them?"

"No, not with the preliminary check. I'll dig a little deeper."

"You know, it's really nice of you to do this," said Agatha. "I don't mean to be taking up so much of your time."

"It's my pleasure," responded Jake. "I'm not busy right now, and what I've done has not taken that much time."

"Okay, if you're sure I'm not imposing too much. I really appreciate it."

"No problem. You have a great day, and if I find anything else, I'll call you."

"Sounds good, and thanks again. Adios."

"Adios."

What an incredibly nice man Jake is, mused Agatha. I liked him when he came to my courtroom. He was always very friendly and polite. I'm really glad we have an opportunity to get better acquainted. Such a coincidence that we are neighbors.

"So, did he learn anything interesting?" Dorothy said as she strolled back into the room.

"Nothing too earth-shattering," replied Agatha. "I'll fill you in while we shop. Are you ready to go?"

"I'm always ready to go shop!"

After an enjoyable morning of shopping in the mall and in the little boutiques close by, Agatha and Dorothy were hungry and found a restaurant near their hotel. As they entered, they saw Ted and Linda also waiting for a table.

"Hi," said Agatha. "Have you had a good morning?"

"Yes," answered Linda. "Better than we could expect, I guess. We spent the morning at the beach with the kids. They wanted to stay, but I've had enough sun."

"Kids never get enough sun," laughed Dorothy.

"So true," agreed Linda.

"Would you like to join us for lunch?" asked Ted.

"We would love to," said Agatha after looking at Dorothy who nodded affirmatively.

They were seated at a lovely outdoor table in the shade.

After they ordered, Dorothy asked how the children were doing.

"Okay," said Linda. "It was such a shock for them. Chelsie saw the shawl floating in the fountain and walked over to pick it up. When she moved it, she saw Marian staring up at her. Of course, when she screamed, Teddy and Stanley ran over to see what she was screaming about and also saw the body. It was pretty ghastly. None of them can get that vision out of their heads. They keep reliving it. Teddy is having nightmares."

"I'm a retired court clerk," said Agatha, "and I've seen many kids involved in some awful situations. It's hard on them at first, but kids are very resilient. They will get over it."

"I'm sure that's true, but it is pretty hard in the meantime," said Linda sadly.

"I should never have let the kids go out at night," said Ted. "I don't know what I was thinking."

"Don't blame yourself," sympathized Dorothy. "It was an accident. There's no way you could have known something so awful would happen and, they might have been the ones to find her even if they had stayed at the hotel all evening. You never know."

"Yes, that's true, I guess," said Ted.

"Did the kids see or hear anyone else?" asked Agatha.

"No, I don't think so," answered Linda.

"Did Rick or Dan say why they weren't with her?" asked Agatha.

"Not really," said Ted. "I heard them tell the police that they walked around with Marian for a little while and then they wanted to go to bed. Marian said she wanted to stay out in the fresh air a little longer and for them to go on in. They feel terrible about the situation and wish they had stayed with her and made sure she got back to her room safely."

"Again, they can't blame themselves," said Dorothy.

"Was she near the fountain when they left her?" asked Agatha.

"They said she was sitting on the edge of the fountain, dangling her hand in the water," said Linda.

"Hmm! How awful!" commented Agatha. "Maybe when she stood to leave she lost her balance. She was pretty drunk."

The others agreed with her.

When their food was served, they switched topics and talked about their upcoming trip to Morocco.

"I can't believe we are going to darkest Africa tomorrow," said Linda. "I still don't know if it's safe."

"Well, I don't think Morocco is exactly the darkest part of Africa," laughed Dorothy, "but it is on the African continent. Lots of tourists go there all the time. It's my understanding you have to be careful or you may get your pocket picked or get taken advantage of by pushy people selling things, but there's nothing really dangerous to worry about."

"Yes, my dear," said Dave winked at his wife. "You must come with me to the Casbah."

"Very funny," said Linda rolling her eyes. "Before we left, I looked up information online about Morocco, and they have had attacks on tourists. They had one last April in Marrakesh."

"We're not going to Marrakesh. We'll be fine, but you can wait for us in Spain if you want to," said Dave.

"No way! We all stay or we all go," responded Linda adamantly.

"Well, the rest of us are going," said Dave.

"Then, I am too," said Linda.

"I'm sure it will be fine," said Dorothy.

"I sincerely hope so," thought Agatha "But, at the rate we're going, I'm not so sure!"

When Agatha and Dorothy got back to the hotel, Katie and Jorha were in the lobby.

"Hi, ladies," said Katie as they walked in.

Jorha gave them a big smile and a little bow.

"Hi, yourselves," said Agatha. "Do you have anyone going on the tour this afternoon?"

"No, it doesn't look like it," said Katie. "Is there any place you ladies would like to go?"

"As a matter of fact," said Dorothy, "I would love to go to Málaga. That's Picasso's birthplace."

"No problem," said Jorha. "I know right where it is. It's less than ten miles away. Do you want to go now?"

"Sure," replied Dorothy. "Will anyone else want to go?"

"Most people are either shopping or spending the day on the beach," said Katie. "You two go ahead."

"Sounds good. Jorha, can you give us fifteen minutes to run up to our room before we leave?" asked Agatha.

"Take your time *señoritas.* I will bring the bus around," said Jorha.

Twenty minutes later, they were on their way. Dorothy gave Agatha some background on Picasso to which both Agatha and Jorha listened intently.

"Fundación Picasso was born in Málaga in October 1891. I'll tell you a funny thing about his birth. As the story goes, Picasso was not breathing when he was born until his uncle blew cigar smoke into his lungs."

"What! Who would do that to a baby?" cried Agatha, which got Jorha laughing.

"I don't know," said Dorothy, "but maybe he panicked and didn't realize he had cigar smoke in his mouth. Anyway, it's just a story and one I imagine Picasso enjoyed telling. He lived in his birth home for the first seventeen months of his life. There is an exhibit of Picasso's ceramics, sculpture, and engravings in the home. After looking there, then, we can move on to the Museo Picasso Málaga, if that is okay with you, Jorha."

"Anything you would like, *señorita,*" said Jorha. "Actually, I believe it's but a short walk from his birthplace to the museum."

"Wonderful! The Museo Picasso Málaga opened in 2003 with the King and Queen of Spain present. On the first day, almost two thousand people visited the museum."

"The museum is rather new, then," said Agatha.

"Yes. There probably would have been one much earlier, but the dictator Franco hated Picasso and said his art was degenerate. Picasso offered to send paintings to Málaga from France in the 1950s, but Franco would not permit it. Much of the collection in the museum came from Picasso's son's wife and from another of his sons after Picasso died. The art is particularly interesting because many of the works were family heirlooms, art Picasso had given to family members, or art he wanted to keep himself. Some of the art had never been on public display before."

"Well, I can hardly wait to view the works with you, Dorothy. Picasso's art has always been an enigma to me," said Agatha.

"I don't know what 'enigma' means, but I've always thought his art was *extrano*," said Jorha.

"What is *extrano*?" asked Agatha.

"I think you would say in English, weird," replied Jorha laughing.

"Well, enigma means non-understandable," laughed Agatha, "but weird works for me."

"Jorha, would you like to walk through the museums with us?" asked Dorothy. "Perhaps I can change the opinions of both of you."

"Yeah! I think I would, if you do not mind," responded Jorha. "And, we are here. Let me park, and we will be the tourists together. Even Jorha."

"Sounds good," laughed Dorothy.

The three had a lovely afternoon and evening, not leaving the museum until it closed at 8:00 p.m. They enjoyed a dinner at a cafe Jorha recommended that specialized in paella. So good.** After dinner they watched a flamenco show in the museum's auditorium. Jorha was a fun companion and he enjoyed being pampered by Dorothy and Agatha, who treated him like a son — or make that a grandson.

They got back to the hotel late, but at about the right time to make their call to Jake, which they did promptly when they returned to their room.

"Buenos dias, Jake," said Agatha when Jake picked up the phone.

"Buenas tardes, Agatha," laughed Jake. "You are becoming quite the Spaniard. Have you had a good day?"

"Another great day, with no disasters," said Agatha.

"That's good," said Jake.

"It's so nice to have your own personal tour guide with you at all times. We went to Picasso's birthplace and museum today, and Dorothy is a fount of knowledge," said Agatha as she smiled at Dorothy, who was sitting on the other bed listening to the conversation.

"That's what happens when you take an art and world history teacher along with you on your travels," said Jake.

"Yup! It's great. Anyway, did you find out any more information," asked Agatha.

"I didn't have a lot of time today. I had to do a project for the police, but I did snag two pieces of very interesting information."

"Good! And what are they?"

"First of all, I know why Jessica is so sad. Her parents were both killed in an automobile accident last year, and the circumstances were suspicious. It appeared that their brakes had been tampered with but nothing came of the investigation. Jessica was supposed to be with them at the time but was ill and couldn't go out that evening. It had to have been a real shock to her and very traumatic. And, by the way, her parents had a big estate. She is a very wealthy young lady."

"Wow!" said Agatha. "Poor little rich girl. She must still be in mourning. What's your second piece of news?"

"Now, this is really interesting. Dave and Diane are from Troy, Ohio, correct?"

"Yes, I believe that's what they said."

"Well, Troy is really a small, podunk town. Most people would know each other."

"Yes, so?"

"Robbie Thomas was born and raised in Troy, Ohio, the same small town the Dixons are from."

# TRAVEL TIPS FROM AGATHA AND DOROTHY

*Hotel Cervantes in Torremolinos, isn't as fancy as some of the other hotels that are on the tour. However, it is so well located, right inside a shopping center, and only a seven-minute walk to the beach; Agatha and Dorothy highly recommend it. The rooms have spacious balconies, many with sea views. During the summer there is a luncheon buffet and barbecue by the pool. Located at 29620 Torremolinos.

**The following is the Spanish Paella recipe Agatha enjoys making for company once they returned home.

### SPANISH PANELLA

Ingredients:

Herb blend:

1 cup chopped fresh parsley

1/4 cup fresh lemon juice

1 tablespoon olive oil

2 large garlic cloves, minced

Paella:

1 cup water

1 teaspoon saffron threads

3 (16 oz.) fat free, low sodium, chicken broth

8 unpeeled jumbo shrimp (about 1/2 lb.)

1 tablespoon olive oil

4 skinned, boned chicken thighs, cut in half (Agatha uses chicken tenders, preferring white meat chicken)

2 links Spanish chorizo sausage (about 6-1/2 oz)

1 (4 oz) slice prosciutto cut into 1 inch pieces

2 cups finely chopped onion

1 cup finely chopped red bell pepper

1 cup canned diced tomatoes, undrained

1 tsp. sweet paprika

3 large garlic cloves, minced

3 cups uncooked Arborio rice or other short-grained rice

1 cup frozen green peas

8 mussels, scrubbed and debearded

1/4 cup fresh lemon juice

Lemon wedges

Directions:

1 - Prepare herb blend by combining ingredients. Set aside.

2 - Prepare paella: combine water, saffron, and broth in large saucepan. Bring to a simmer (do not boil). Keep warm over low heat. Peel and devein shrimp, leaving tails intact. Set aside.

3 - Heat 1 tablespoon oil in large skillet over medium high heat. Add chicken, sauté 2 minutes on each side. Remove from pan. Add shrimp and sauté 2 minutes. Remove from pan. Add sausage and prosciutto, sauté 2 minutes. Remove from pan. Reduce heat to medium low. Add onion and bell pepper; sauté 15 minutes, stirring occasionally. Add tomatoes, paprika, and 3 garlic cloves; cook 5 minutes. Add rice; cook 1 minute, stirring constantly. Stir in herb blend, broth mixture, chicken, sausage mixture and peas. Bring to a low boil; cook 10 minutes, stirring

frequently. Add mussels to pan, nestling them into rice mixture. Cook 5 minutes or until shells open; discard any unopened shells. Arrange shrimp, heads down, in rice mixture and cook 5 minutes until shrimp are done. Sprinkle with 1/4 cup lemon juice. Remove from heat, cover with a towel and let stand 10 minutes. Serve with lemon wedges.

# CHAPTER 8

## *Day 8*

---

*This morning we will take a short drive to Algeciras
for the ferry ride across the Strait of Gibraltar, where
the Atlantic meets the Mediterranean. Landing in
North Africa, we take another short drive to the exotic
Moroccan city of Tétouan. We will visit the Casbah
and enjoy a Moroccan feast with local entertainment
before returning to Spain. Of course, there will be plenty
of time to shop!*

---

"Good morning," said Katie as she boarded the bus. She was always the last to board, making sure that all the tour members boarded before her and that their luggage was loaded.

"This is my favorite day on the tour," she said. "We are going to enter a world that is very foreign and exotic to most of us."

"And safe, right?" said Linda worriedly.

"And safe," agreed Katie. "Our tours have never had any problems while visiting Morocco. No need to worry. We have a short ride to catch the ferry so we can cross the Strait of Gibraltar to North Africa."

"I hope I don't get seasick," frowned Rick.

"You know, I have never had a tour member get seasick. I think the ride is too short, less than an hour," said Katie.

"Tell my stomach that," quipped Rick.

"I think she better tell your inner ear," commented Diane as she turned to look at Rick. "That's where the trouble comes from. I have some pills for seasickness if you would like one. I took one this morning before we left the hotel. Do you want one?"

"Sure, thanks," said Rick.

"Anyone else?" asked Diane.

The other passengers just shook their heads or murmured no.

Actually, the trip on the high-speed ferry across the Strait of Gibraltar was short, beautiful, and uneventful. No one had to dash to the bathroom or to the side of the ferry because of seasickness, and all of the travelers were in a much better mood by the time they reached the shore than they had been when they first started out that morning.

"Wow!" exclaimed Dorothy as she exited the bus. "This place looks, sounds, and smells exotic. Doesn't it?"

"Yes, it certainly does," replied Agatha, looking around with wide eyes. "How cool is this!"

The travelers were immediately bombarded with hawkers selling their wares. Katie had warned them not to buy anything when they first got off the ferry, but to wait until they were in town.

It was all so exciting! It felt different here then on the European side. Here there were people in African garb, camels upon which tourists could ride, and even a snake charmer demonstrating his unusual talent. Agatha took the opportunity to have her picture taken with the snake around her neck. Dorothy said, "No way!"

Dorothy just wanted to sit down and sketch everything in sight, but Katie hurried them along to their modern air-conditioned bus for the ride to the Moroccan city of Tangier. Agatha was snapping pictures right and left so Dorothy knew she could use Agatha's pictures to refresh her memory later for drawings.

Once they were settled and on their way, Katie began her narrative about the day that was ahead.

"One of the main activities of this tour is—drumroll please—shopping!"

Several male groans could be heard.

"Oh, don't despair, gentleman. There will be much that you will enjoy, and you may even want to purchase a few bargains. There are many handcrafted Moroccan goods for sale, such as babouche slippers, woodworks, brass works, ironworks, bronze works, jewelry, kaftans, carpets, and pottery. You may also be interested in the spices, which Moroccans use in their cooking and also use for medicinal purposes. We'll meet a traditional herbalist at the souk we'll be visiting this morning, and the spices and herbs will be available for sale."

"What's a souk?" asked Teddy, his eyes wide with excitement. "And, will I get to ride on a camel? Mom wouldn't let me hold the snake."

"Chances are good that you will get to ride a camel, Teddy, and a souk is an outdoor market. You know, like a farmer's market at home. We'll also shop at a typical bazaar this afternoon. A bazaar is in an enclosed area with goods for sale. Remember, never purchase anything at the first price offered. It's expected that you'll bargain, and you'll pay way over value if you don't participate in the native tradition of haggling.* In between the shopping, you will enjoy a walking tour of the Medina, which is the old quarter, and the *Casbah*, which is the old fortress. You'll see some of Morocco's rich and beautiful architecture. On the walking tour, we'll see a snake charmer and visit a bakery so you can try some of the local bread, which is very good. We will have a late lunch at a traditional Moroccan restaurant where you will be entertained by a Berber dancer."

"What's a Berber or was that a barber?" asked Dave.

"That's Berber, and I'm so glad you asked," smiled Katie. "Two of every three Moroccans are Berbers. They're thought to be descendants of people of mixed origins and do not make up a homogeneous race. They have survived many invasions, and have very strong tribal and family ties. The women often paint themselves with henna in elaborate patterns. You may have seen pictures. They believe that this not only makes them beautiful but also protects them from evil spirits. You'll hear more about Berbers at lunch."

"We'll also make a short stop at Cape Spartel," continued Katie "where the Atlantic Ocean meets the Mediterranean Sea. Below the cape are the Caves of Hercules. It's a very beautiful area. We'll have a taste of traditional mint tea there and learn about the mint tea ritual.** Their mint tea is made with a tea called gun powder green tea, which does contain a low dose of caffeine. Agatha, I know you and Dorothy love herb tea, but without caffeine, so we can arrange for mint tea without the green tea."

"Thank you," said Agatha.

"Green tea has a lot of antioxidants, you know," said Linda, "which is very good for you."

"I know," agreed Agatha. "We just don't do caffeine. You may not either when you are our age and have high blood pressure."

"I can't ever imagine doing without my caffeine," said Linda. "I could never get going in the morning without it."

"Anyway," continued Katie, "we will end our day with a visit to the Caves of Hercules and a stop at an Atlantic dune, where you may ride a camel if you want to."

"Oh boy," exclaimed Teddy. "I want to ride a camel. Can I, mom? Please! Please!"

"I think that would be okay," said Linda. "How much is it, Katie?"

"It's part of the tour," said Katie. "No extra charge."

"Are you going to ride a camel, Agatha," asked Dorothy looking a little unsure that she herself would ride.

"Are you kidding? Of course!" exclaimed Agatha. "When will we ever get another opportunity to ride a real camel?"

"That's true," said Dorothy still looking a little skeptical. "Or, you could ride and I could take your picture and sketch you on the camel."

"We'll see," returned Agatha. She was pretty sure she could talk Dorothy into it when the time came.

About eight hours later the time had come to make that decision. All tour members had really enjoyed their day. Much money had been spent, lots of food eaten, and their feet ached from walking.

"Okay," said Agatha, turning to Dorothy as the bus pulled up to a stop at the Atlantic dune. "It's decision time."

"Oh dear," replied Dorothy looking out the window at the camels lined up along a rope. "They are so big, and they smell really bad. You sit up really high. What if you fall off?"

"I'm sure you're strapped in safely. Come on! You can't miss this opportunity. What do you think, Katie? Are we too old to ride a camel?"

"Are you kidding? You two? No way," said Katie. "And, if you both go, I think everyone else will go, too."

"Yeah, we would shame them into it," said Agatha with a sly look on her face. "If the two old ladies can go, they certainly can go too."

"Oh, okay," said Dorothy reluctantly. "What the heck! You only live once, and you're right Agatha, I may never have this opportunity again. I just hope I don't fall off, break a leg, and be a cripple for the rest of my life."

"Don't be silly," said Agatha. "Come on. It will be fun. Just hang on tight."

All of the tour members were soon mounted on camels and moseying down the trail with the guide in the lead and Katie coming up behind.

"It's so quiet," remarked David.

"That's because camels do not have hooves nor are they shoed like horses," said the English-speaking guide. "That coupled with the fact that most of the time they are walking on sand makes your ride very quiet."

"With the heat and the sway of the camel gait, I may end up asleep and then fall off," commented Dorothy, but no longer afraid.

"No way," said Teddy who was on the camel just in front of Dorothy. "This is too fun. I can hardly wait to tell my friends at home about this. Dad, turn around and take my picture."

Ted, who was riding just in front of Teddy, twisted around on his seat and snapped a couple of shots. "You look great on that camel, son," he said.

"I'm an Arabian prince going to rescue a fair maiden," said Teddy. He tried to get his camel to go faster but the camel didn't seem to know what 'giddy-up' meant and continued to plod along.

"I'm glad we did this at the end of the day when the sun is going down," called out Diane from farther up the line of camels. "Even so, it's still really hot!"

"Yup, it is that, but this is so fun," answered Dorothy. "Thank you for talking me into riding, Agatha."

"You're welcome," said Agatha. "That's what a friend is for."

The ride was coming to an end, and the camels in the front were kneeling down so their riders could disembark.

"I'll be lucky not to go over on my head," thought Agatha as she watched the camels in front of her; but when her turn came, she leaned back as her camel went forward as instructed, and she managed to hang on so she could slide off the side.

Everyone was laughing and talking excitedly. Agatha watched Dorothy slide off her camel gracefully with a big smile on her face.

"That was so much fun," enthused Dorothy. "I'm so proud of myself for doing that."

"I'm proud of you for doing it too," laughed Agatha.

"Where did Katie go?" asked Agatha. "She was right behind you. Did she pass you by?"

"No," answered Dorothy. "I didn't see her, but then I was concentrating on how I was going to get off the camel. I don't know where she went."

The group had gathered around a table upon which was displayed the pictures that had been professionally taken of the camel riders as they began their ride.

Jorha had pulled the bus up near the group so they could board after they purchased their pictures.

"Where's Katie?" asked Jorha as he strolled over to Agatha and Dorothy.

"I don't know. We were just wondering the same thing," Agatha said as she looked over the pictures. "She had been riding behind Dorothy but wasn't there when the ride ended."

"Look," said Dorothy. "There's a lot of hubbub going on over there with the camels."

She was right. One Moroccan was yelling at another one, and another man was running up and down the line of camels.

"I'll go see what is going on," said Jorha as he hurried over to the man who had been the guide for the ride.

As he approached, the Moroccan who had been yelling at someone else began yelling at Jorha that one of his camels was missing.

When the tour group members finished purchasing their pictures, they boarded the bus, which was idling with the air conditioner running, so they could wait for Jorha and Katie.

About fifteen minutes later, Jorha boarded the bus alone and shut the door.

"Where's Katie," Rick called out.

"She will be along later," answered Jorha. "We must go so as not to miss the ferry."

One look at Jorha, and Agatha knew something was very wrong. She had a feeling that not only was a camel missing but, so was Katie.

# TRAVEL TIPS FROM AGATHA AND DOROTHY

*You must bargain when in Morocco. Never, never pay the first price quoted. You are expected to bargain for everything, from vegetables to hotel rooms. The goal is for the seller to make a profit and and the buyer to pay the best price. It is a game between buyer and seller so keep smiling throughout.

**Green mint tea is the national drink, and is the symbol of hospitality. It is considered very ill-mannered to refuse it, although they usually understand if it is declined because of medical or religious reasons. The tea ceremony is performed for guests according to strict rules. The mint tea is served in small, slender glasses decorated with a beautiful filigree pattern.

# CHAPTER 9

## Day 9

*Costa del sol—Gibraltar—Seville: A visit to the British city of Gibraltar will start our day with a tour of the famed Rock, then on to visit St. Michael's Cave and a chance to meet the Barbary apes! Back into Spain, we continue through the vineyards of Jerez, home of sherry. We will have a two-night stay in Seville, Andalusia's most beautiful city. Tonight we shall experience an authentic Andalusian flamenco show.*

There had been no phone call in the middle of the night this time, but that didn't mean Agatha and Dorothy had a good night's sleep. A phone call from Katie would have been welcome. How could Katie and a camel disappear?

It was very early when Agatha gave up trying to sleep and got up.

"Good morning," said Dorothy groggily. "I'm glad you got up. I've been lying here awake for a long time."

"Good morning," responded Agatha. "I know what you mean. I did not sleep much last night. I wonder if Katie has returned."

"I don't know. Shall we call down to see if we can get a pot of hot water so we can drink some tea while we get ready?"

"Good idea. After we get dressed and packed, it should be late enough to call Jorha to see if he has heard anything new," Agatha said as she stepped into the bathroom to take her shower.

Forty-five minutes later they were both ready and packed. First, Agatha dialed Katie's number, but it went to her voice mail. Then she called Jorha.

"*Buenos dias,*" answered Jorha.

"Good morning, Jorha," said Agatha. "Have you heard anything from Katie?"

"*Nada,* not a word," said Jorha worriedly. "The authorities, they look for her."

"Yes. Hopefully, we'll hear something soon. How could she just disappear?" wondered Agatha aloud. "She was right there with us."

"*Si,* I don't know," said Jorha. "We continue today, then I know not what to do."

"How far is Seville," asked Agatha.

"About one hundred and fifty kilometers," replied Jorha.

"Okay. We'll see you at the bus at eight."

"Right. *Adios!*"

Agatha looked up at Dorothy and said, "Jorha hasn't heard anything. He will continue the tour as planned today. Then, he's not sure what to do."

"Oh my word," said Dorothy. "I'm so worried about her. Well, let's go down to breakfast and try to eat something before we leave?"

"Yeah, we better eat, even though I don't feel like it. Let's go."

Many of the tour members were having breakfast as Agatha and Dorothy finished another cup of tea with toast and fruit. The Johnson family was running a bit late and hurried into the breakfast room.

"Good morning," they all said as they greeted the others. Teddy headed right for the food and began filling a plate. The rest of the family paused at Agatha and Dorothy's table.

"Have you heard anything about Katie," asked Linda.

"No," responded Agatha. "I called Jorha this morning, and he hadn't heard a thing. He said the authorities were looking for her."

"How could she disappear on a camel ride?" queried Ted.

"I knew it wasn't safe going to Africa," said Linda. "The rest of us are lucky to come back alive."

"Now Linda," said Ted as he put his arm around her.

Chelsie was quiet as she stood next to her mother and still looked to be in shock from her previous experience of finding Marian.

"Ted, do you have your camera with you," asked Agatha.

"Sure do," answered Ted as he pulled it out of the deep pocket of his jacket. "Do you want me to take your picture?"

"No, no, not right now, but could I see the picture you took of Teddy yesterday on the camel ride?" asked Agatha.

"Of course! Let me find it for you," Ted said as he fiddled with the camera.

"Here it is. It's a pretty good picture in spite of the movement of the camels."

Ted passed the camera to Agatha.

"It is a good picture and look! You can see Katie in the picture at the end of the line," Dorothy said as she peered over Agatha's shoulder.

"Yes. It looks like she's stopped and talking to someone," said Agatha.

"Let's see," said Ted as he looked closely at the picture. "You're right! There is someone with her in the picture."

"We need to get this to the authorities in Morocco," said Agatha excitedly. "And could you email it to me, too?"

Just then Jorha entered the breakfast room.

"Everyone! *Atencion*," said Jorha loudly. "I just got a call from Katie. She is good. She is all right. I am so happy."

Everyone cheered with delight at his announcement and began talking excitedly.

"Thank goodness," said Agatha. "What happened to her?"

"She said she would tell us when she meets with us in Gibraltar. She takes the ferry there," explained Jorha, who was grinning from ear to ear.

"Let's all finish the breakfast so we can go. She will be in Gibraltar at eleven. We can do our sightseeing before this time," said Jorha.

They were soon loaded on the bus and on their way.

"*Señorita* Dorothy," said Jorha once they were on the road. "Do you know anything about Gibraltar that you could tell the tour members?"

"Well, I think I remember a bit about its history, and I've been reading my tour book" answered Dorothy as she reluctantly assumed the position that Katie usually held when she spoke to the group.

"Jorha has asked me to speak to you about Gibraltar. Please feel free to chime in at any time," said Dorothy. "This isn't really my field of expertise."

"I'm sure you know more than the rest of us," said Rick.

"Well, we shall see about that," Dorothy began. "There are two unique things about Gibraltar, I think. The first, of course, is that it's a small piece of Britain surrounded by Spain. When I say small, I mean small. The guidebook says it is three miles long and three-quarters of a mile wide, two point six square miles. It's really just a narrow peninsula with a big rock and is connected to Spain by a sandy isthmus a mile long. From Gibraltar the Brits guard the Strait of Gibraltar, which is the only entrance to the Mediterranean Sea from the Atlantic Ocean and so it's important for trading purposes. The second thing that is unique about Gibraltar is the two hundred Barbary monkeys that inhabit the rock."

"Monkeys," exclaimed Teddy. "We're going to see monkeys?"

"Up close and personal," laughed Stanley. "I've been to the rock before, and those monkeys are a bunch of little rascals."

"Please tell us about the monkeys, Stanley, since you've actually seen them," encouraged Dorothy.

"Okay," said Stanley. "I remember that they think they're human, they're very comfortable around people, and they don't frighten off easily. They're pretty good-sized, around thirty-five pounds. Everyone thinks they're cute until one of them does something naughty, and they can be very naughty. All I can say is, hang on to your belongings. They have been known to grab and run with purses and cameras while other monkeys cheer them on. I saw a monkey grab an ice cream cone out of the hand of a child and run off with it. It was like the other monkeys were laughing as the little boy broke into tears. The monkeys can be real problems, and the locals are not particularly fond of them. Most of the time, they're friendly, too friendly, but, we were warned they can turn vicious, especially if their babies are threatened."

"Teddy, you are to stay away from them," his mom said to him sternly.

"Oh, mom! I'll stay with Chelsie and Stanley," responded Teddy. "They'll protect me."

"Why do they keep them on the island if they are such a problem?" asked Nancy. "Because they're a tourist attraction?"

"Well, as I understand it, believe it or not, it's because of a superstition," answered Stanley. "There is a legend that, as long as Gibraltar has Barbary monkeys, it will remain under British rule. In fact, they say that during the Second World War, there were only about seven monkeys on the island and British Prime Minister Winston Churchill ordered more monkeys to be brought from Morocco and Algeria. That's why there are so many of them on the rock today. Anyway, that's about all I know about the famous monkeys of Gibraltar."

"I don't know much more either," said Dorothy.

"What's at St. Michael's Cave?" asked Rick. "Someone at home said we should see it, if we can."

"I don't really know," said Dorothy. "Let's see what the guidebook says."

"Hmm," Dorothy said as she looked at the travel book Agatha handed her. "It says, this is one of a network of limestone caves. They were even mentioned in the writings of Roman visitors before the time of Christ. At one time, the caves were thought to be bottomless, and one cave was thought to be the undersea link to Africa through which the original Barbary apes came."

Dorothy said that was all she knew and took her seat.

"*Gracias, Señorita* Dorothy and *Señor* Stanley," said Jorha as he stopped the bus. "We are now at the Gibraltar. Your timing, she is good. You have the free time until half past noon hour. Be back to the bus at twelve-thirty, *por favor*. Oh, and be sure to eat de lunch before you return."

"And look at all de shops before we return" Dorothy said teasingly as she imitated Jorha's accent and stepped off the bus.

Agatha, too, stepped down and looked around. "I don't know about you, but I'm interested in shopping and in the monkeys, not so interested in the cave."

"I agree," said Dorothy. "I have seen lots of caves in the United States."

"Okay, let's look at the monkeys and walk around their area, then we'll hit the shops. I would like to go to Gibraltar Crystal Factory, where you can see the crystal being made."*

"Me, too," said Dorothy, "and I understand they have an English Marks and Spencer department store and several book stores, with books in English. Imagine that! I bet they have some good English mysteries. We could use a new stash of books to read."

By 11:30 a.m., Dorothy and Agatha were sitting at the House of Sacarello** eating lunch, having experienced the monkeys and having shopped their hearts out at the British shops.

"I thought English food was supposed to be bad. This soup is tasty, the salad is very fresh, and the scones are to die for," said Agatha.

"You bet," agreed Dorothy, as she took a big bite of a scone, slathered with clotted cream and raspberry jam. "Hmmm, so good."

"Maybe I can get a scone recipe to take home," said Agatha looking around for someone to ask.

"Good plan. They also have some boxed mixes for scones up front."

"I'm sure scratch would be better."

"I hope Katie got back," said Dorothy.

"Me, too! I guess we'll know when we get back to the bus."

"True," agreed Agatha.

"You know, I've been thinking," continued Agatha. "There is nothing on the schedule for tomorrow night. Maybe we should sit down with Katie and Jorha and go over all the information we have and think about everything we have observed. We can read through my journal and look at your sketches. Maybe something will pop out at us that we have missed. I hope we can go over everything with Jake, too."

"That's a good idea. We'll put on our thinking caps. Please pass the jam."

Soon they were strolling down the street toward the meeting place for the bus. Their tummies were full, and Agatha had a recipe*** for real English scones tucked away in her purse. About a block from the bus, Teddy came running up to them shouting, "Did you see the monkeys? Did you see the monkeys?"

"Yes," laughed Dorothy. "We saw the monkeys. I take it you did, too."

"We sure did!" laughed Teddy. "One of them grabbed Mom's guidebook and ripped it to shreds. It was so cool! You should have seen her face."

"Your Mom's face or the monkey's," asked Agatha with a big smile.

"Both," giggled Teddy.

Ted and Linda were laughing, too, as they walked up behind Teddy. It was good to see the stress eliminated from Linda's face.

"It looks like you've had a good time," said Dorothy.

"We did," smiled Linda. "Those crazy monkeys were crazy."

"Teddy said you got up close and personal with one of the monkeys," smiled Agatha.

"Unfortunately, yes. We had to buy a new guidebook since ours was confiscated by my new friend. Thank goodness there were book stores here, with books in English," said Linda.

"The King's English," said Ted, "or is it the Queen's English these days?"

"The caves were really neat, too," said Teddy.

"We didn't see you on the cave tour," said Ted to Agatha and Dorothy. "Did you find something else more fun to do?"

"Shopping," said Agatha, looking a little embarrassed. For some reason, she felt a little guilty about choosing to shop over sightseeing.

But Linda was interested, and said, "Hmmm, that sounds fun. What did you find?"

"I got some British wool yarn so I can knit a sweater," said Agatha.

"And I bought a British wool sweater, already made up," said Dorothy. "I don't knit, yet, anyway. Agatha has always promised to teach me."

"I wish I could knit. Knitting's really in now," said Chelsie as she joined the group with Stanley.

"I would be happy to teach you," said Agatha. "The store where I bought the yarn is just down the block. Shall we run down and get a skein of yarn and some needles so I can teach you on the bus? You can knit a scarf."

"Oh, fun!" exclaimed Chelsie. "Let's do it."

"I might as well get some now, too," said Dorothy. "No time like the present to learn."

"Can I join the knitting group?" asked Linda.

"Sure. We'll do a regular class. Actually, knitting is a fun thing to do while riding on the bus. Once you are comfortable with the basic stitch, you can knit and still look out the window a lot. And knitting is very relaxing. It has something to do with the repetitive actions, I'm told. Very soothing."

"I'm sold. Let's go," said Linda.

The females of the group all walked back to the yarn shop, and Agatha helped each one choose some yarn and buy needles of the proper size. It took a little longer than they expected because Chelsie had an especially difficult time making up her mind about the yarn, so they had to hurry to catch the bus. Agatha and Dorothy, lagging a bit behind, were both breathing hard as they boarded.

Agatha looked up expectantly as her head came up high enough to see the first seat.

"Hi!" laughed Katie. "You didn't have to run. We would have waited for you."

"Katie!" I'm so glad to see you," said Agatha as she threw her arms around her. "We were so worried about you. Are you okay?"

"I'm fine," Katie said as she gave Agatha and then Dorothy a hug. "I just had a bit of an adventure. I'll tell you all about it later."

"So, did they find the camel, too?" asked Dorothy.

"Yes, the camel was returned safe and sound, also. The camel and I became very good friends," said Katie with a grin.

"I hear you are going to give a knitting lesson," said Katie. "I wish I had some yarn. I have always wanted to learn to knit."

"Actually, you may be able to talk Chelsie out of some of her yarn. She couldn't make up her mind, so she bought two different colored skeins."

"All right, Chelsie, how about it? Are you willing to sell some yarn to me?" asked Katie.

"Sure," replied Chelsie. "Tell you what. I'll let you choose which one you like the best and I will do the other one. Pink or purple?"

"They're both pretty," said Katie as she fingered the yarn. "I think pink. Okay?"

"Pink huh!" said Chelsie frowning.

"Okay, I'll take purple," laughed Katie.

"No, no. Pink is fine. My mind is made up," Chelsie said resolutely.

"Great, and I've got some extra needles," said Agatha. "Let's all meet at the back of the bus once we are out of the town and on the highway."

"It's about a two-hour drive to Seville," said Katie.

"That will give you plenty of time to learn the basic stitch called the garter stitch," said Agatha.

"Hey! How come we're left out?" asked Lora, who had been listening to the conversation.

"Yeah! We want to learn to knit too," joined in Nancy.

"Oh, I'm sorry. You two weren't around when we purchased the yarn. But, I'm sure there will be a yarn shop in Seville. We'll get you some there, and get you started tomorrow. Will you be off with relatives in Seville?" asked Agatha.

"Hmm, actually yes. Rubio has a cousin there, doesn't he, Nancy?" asked Lora.

"Uh, yes," responded Nancy, glancing at her husband. "But we can probably find a yarn shop before we visit."

"Good, then we will get you started tomorrow," said Agatha. "Buy one skein of yarn like this one and size eight needles. Oh, let's see, that's US size. Get five-mm needles. The shopkeeper will probably know and can help you."

"We have our book to read in the meantime," said Nancy.

"Yeah. *Don Quixote* is a very, very long book," added Lora.

"So true," agreed Nancy.

"Jessica, do you want to learn to knit, or do you already know how?" asked Agatha.

"No. I'm fine," Jessica said, but was looking at all the colorful yarns a bit wistfully. "The yarns are very pretty."

"Why don't you give it a try?" urged Dorothy.

"No. I've tried it before and didn't like it." Jessica turned away from the group and stared out the window.

"What about you, Diane?" Agatha asked.

"No thanks. I've tried it before too, and I'm just too uncoordinated."

"Okay. I guess we have our knitting group."

Jorha started up the bus, and off they went. Two hours later, four scarves in various colors had been started.

"This will be a neat souvenir if I can ever get it done," said Linda as Agatha assisted her in picking up a dropped stitch.

"You'll get it done if you are tenacious," said Agatha. "Pretty soon this simple knit stitch will be second nature."

"This is so cool," said Chelsie as she concentrated on what she was doing. So far she had not dropped a single stitch and seemed to have a knack for knitting.

"I have to stop to give my Seville spiel," said Katie as she stood and stretched. She carried her knitting to the front of the bus and put it in her travel bag before picking up the microphone.

Many of the men were napping and woke up groggily as Katie announced that they were entering the outskirts of Seville.

"We will soon arrive in Seville, a city known for its romance and beauty. It was made famous by Mozart and Bizet in their operas of *Don Giovanni* and *Carmen,* respectively."

"Ah, the city of Don Juan," said Stanley.

"Yes, it is," agreed Katie. "We will be spending the night at a small boutique hotel call Alcoba del Rey de Sevilla.**** We'll have more than half of the rooms in this lovely small hotel. All the rooms open onto a central Andalusian patio. Each room has a name and a unique decor, so you may want to visit each other's rooms. In addition, guests may purchase anything they see in the hotel, even furnishings. So it's not only a boutique hotel but also a hotel boutique and antique store."

"That sounds fun," said Dorothy.

"I think you will all enjoy it. Dinner is on your own, but we will meet in the lobby at 9:00 p.m. to go to a flamenco show at El Patio Sevillano*****."

"We have other plans tonight," said Rick, "so don't wait for us."

"You will miss a good show," said Katie.

"I'm sure, but we'll see you in the morning," responded Rick.

"Okay," said Katie. "One warning. Unfortunately there's a lot of crime in Seville. Guard your purses, your wallets, and your cameras especially, and stay in well-lit areas with lots of people. That won't be hard to do. There are a lot of people in Seville."

"Agatha, you may want to learn to dance the *Las Sevillanas* and play the castanets," said Katie.

"You bet. I'm game," said Agatha. "I definitely want to take some castanets home with me."

"Those will be useful," smiled Dorothy.

Jorha parked the bus in front of the hotel, and the group traipsed off. Agatha took the opportunity to tell Katie that she wanted to hear the whole story of Katie's missing the ferry from Morocco. Katie said they could have dinner together and made arrangements to meet at 6:00 p.m. in Agatha and Dorothy's room.

Agatha and Dorothy were settled in their room and dressed for the evening when Katie knocked on their door.

"Hi," Katie said when Dorothy opened the door.

"Hi! Come on in," said Dorothy.

"Thanks! Do you two want to go out to eat or shall I have Jorha bring some food in?" asked Katie.

"Bringing food in sounds like a good idea since we're going out later tonight," said Agatha.

"Sounds good to me, too," said Dorothy.

"Good. I was hoping you would say that," said Katie. "We have a favorite place called El Fogon de Lena.* We often order from there while in Seville. I'll send Jorha for the food. Will you trust him to choose your dinner?"

Both Agatha and Dorothy heartily agreed, that they would.

"OK, let me call him right quick," Katie said as she picked up the room phone.

"Jorha, they're game," Katie said into the phone. "Pick up the food, and we'll eat in my room since I have a table. Be sure to get some fresh fruit tarts for dessert. Thanks."

They went through the patio to Katie's room to wait for Jorha.

Once they had settled down in the sitting area, Agatha said, "Okay! Out with it. What happened to you and the camel."

"Well, basically the camel ran away with me," said Katie.

"What! Who was the guy talking to you just before it happened? Ted took a picture of Teddy, and we could see you had stopped and were talking to someone in the picture." said Agatha.

"Yes. A man stopped me, and apparently something was wrong with the camel's hoof. The man was checking it out and telling me something, but I couldn't understand what he was saying since he wasn't speaking English. When he finished, he whacked the rear of the camel and the camel took off, but not in the right direction. The man yelled and waved his arms but that seemed to make the camel go faster. I figured the man would tell someone, and they would come after me; but apparently he told no one. I guess he thought he would get in trouble."

"So how did you get back?" asked Dorothy.

"Well, the camel kept going deeper into the desert. I couldn't get him to stop or get him to turn around, but we finally reached a deserted place—I guess like an oasis. There were palm trees and a little building. The camel laid down and about threw me off over its head. Anyway, I got off the darn thing, none too gracefully. My phone wouldn't work out there, and I had no idea where I was. I couldn't find any water in the oasis. I would have been afraid to drink it even if there had been some. All I had was one water bottle in my back pack and the water was going fast. I was pretty scared."

"I bet you were," sympathized Agatha.

"I decided that I better stay where I was. I assumed people would eventually be looking for me and I didn't know what else to do. I wasn't even sure which way to go if I started walking. Around midnight a caravan of off-road vehicles came by the oasis. I was scared of who they might be, but I was more scared of being left out in the desert alone, especially during the heat of the day with very little water. Anyway, I decided I better flag them down, and they turned out to be a bunch of Brits on vacation. They took me and the camel back to the camel line."

"Wow! What an adventure," exclaimed Dorothy.

"You can say that again," sighed Katie.

"Yeah! Another weird occurrence that could have ended in a disaster, even a death," remarked Agatha.

# TRAVEL TIPS FROM AGATHA AND DOROTHY

*Gibraltar has quite a few crystal shops, many of which are just off Main Street.

**House of Sacarello, 57 Irish Town. This is the oldest coffee house restaurant in Gibraltar. Great food!

***British Scone recipe

## BRITISH SCONES

Ingredients:

2 cups all-purpose flour

1 teaspoon cream of tartar

1/2 teaspoon baking soda

1 pinch salt

1/4 cup margarine

1/8 cup white sugar (you may like it a little sweeter so add a little more sugar if desired)

1/2 cup milk

2 tablespoons milk

(You can add raisins, currents or cranberries - about1 cup)

Directions:

1. Preheat oven to 425 degrees F. Line a baking sheet with parchment paper.

2. Sift the flour, cream of tartar, baking soda, and salt into a bowl.

3. Rub in the butter until the mixture resembles fine breadcrumbs. Stir in the sugar and enough milk to mix to a soft dough.

4. Turn onto a floured surface, knead lightly and roll out to a 3/4-inch thickness. Cut into 2-inch rounds and place on the prepared baking sheet. Brush with milk to glaze.

Bake at 425 degrees F for 10-15 minutes then cool on a wire rack. Serve with butter or clotted cream and jam.

****Hotel Alcoba de Rey de Sevilla, 41009 Sevilla, www.alcobadelrey. com, tel. (95-491-58-0). The guests can buy everything they see in the hotel, even the beds and furnishings.

*****El Patio Sevillano, Paseo de Cristóbal Colón 11, www.elpatiose-villano.com, (tel. 95-421-41-20).

# CHAPTER 10

## Day 10

Seville: Today we shall see the splendors of Seville, including the wonders of seven hundred years of influence by the Moors. We will visit the Palace of Alcázar, the old district of Santa Cruz and visit the tomb of Christopher Columbus, located in Spain's largest Gothic Cathedral. We'll end the tour at Parque de Maria Luisa where you will enjoy a horse and carriage ride. Your evening will be free.

Last night Agatha and Dorothy had a delicious dinner with Katie and Jorha, and later, greatly enjoyed the floorshow of flamenco music and dancing. They were so glad they got to see this type of show three times. They were all different and it was hard to say which show was best, but it was fun to enjoy last night's show with their tour friends.

Since they had spent the early evening talking only about Katie's camel experience they all decided to meet again tonight and go over everything strange that has happened on the trip, and to review all the information that they had gotten from Jake to see if any theory emerges. But, in the meantime, Agatha and Dorothy were going to enjoy their day in Seville.

The group gathered after a late breakfast and boarded their bus for the day's tour. Missing, as was often the case, were the Garcias and the Zimmermans who were visiting relatives again. Jessica, however, had decided to join the group today, although she looked even more haggard than usual. Agatha saw Diane eyeing her, and was pretty sure that Diane would take Jessica under her wing again. Time to sit back and relax, and enjoy the day.

It was good to have Katie in her usual spot, so all could enjoy her knowledge and enthusiasm. She had explained what had happened with her camel to the whole group at breakfast.

"Good morning again, everyone," said Katie. "Are you all ready for a day of touring beautiful Seville?"

Everyone agreed that they were ready.

"Before we start, I do need to know if any of you wish to attend a bullfight.* Jorha will get tickets for today if you wish to attend. Anyone?"

"Oh boy! I want to go," said Teddy.

"No, I don't think so," said his Dad. "I understand the tickets are really pricey and the fight pretty gruesome."

"It is pricey. The fight itself is a matter of personal taste." said Katie. "Some consider it an art form."

"And some consider it disgusting," said Chelsie.

No one else spoke up.

"Okay," continued Katie, "hearing no takers, on with the day. Seville is Spain's fourth largest city and one of its most beautiful. We'll begin our tour of Seville at the fourteenth- century Alcázar, the oldest royal residence in Europe that's still in use. King Juan Carlos and Queen Sofia stay here when visiting Seville. It was originally a Moorish fort but much of it was built by Peter the Cruel, also known as Pedro I of Castile or Peter the Just. Obviously a matter of opinion."

"Just like bull fighting," commented Chelsie. "All depends on who's looking at it."

"Very astute!" said Katie and then continued. "You'll find the Alcázar somewhat reminiscent of the Alhambra. Particularly look for the dome in the Hall of Ambassadors and the Maiden's Court. The Maiden's Court is so named because of the legend that the Moors demanded one hundred virgins every year as a tribute from Christian kingdoms in Iberia."

"Wow! A new batch every year!" exclaimed Ken as the men chuckled and the women frowned.

"That's disgusting," said Diane. "Not funny!"

"What's a virgin?" asked Teddy.

"Later," said his Dad.

"Well, it's thought to be just a myth," said Katie with a smile, "but who knows. From there we will go to the old district of Santa Cruz, Seville. This is the primary tourist area. It's the former Jewish quarter of medieval Seville. The Alhambra Decree of 1492, the year Columbus sailed the ocean blue as mentioned before, expelled the Jews from Spain. It's kind of ironic that the Jews lived in relative peace and prosperity under Moorish rule, but were expelled under Christian rule. Dorothy, you may want to visit *Iglesia de Santa Cruz en Calle Mateos Gago* on *Calle Mateos Gago* Street. It houses a painting of the Last Supper by Santa Cruz native Bartolomé Esteban Murillo. Also the *Museo de Bellas Artes* has a gallery devoted to Murillo."

"Yes. I am planning on seeing them, thank you," responded Dorothy.

"When I'm finished will you tell us a little more about Murillo, Dorothy?" asked Katie.

"Of course," answered Dorothy.

"Good, thank you," continued Katie. "I think you all will enjoy Santa Cruz. It's a labyrinth of very old narrow streets. One of the streets was once the home of Washington Irving."

"Oh, that's so sad," said Linda. "I remember talking about Washington Irving with Marian."

Everyone nodded their heads, remembering the conversation on the bus as they had approached Toledo.

"Yes," agreed Katie. "She probably would have had another book for us to read. Anyway, after our stop at Santa Cruz, we'll proceed to *Catedral de Sevilla*\*\* and La *Giralda* Tower. This cathedral is the largest Gothic building in the world and the third-largest church in Europe, after St. Peter's in Rome and St. Paul's in London. Construction was started in the late thirteenth century on the site of a mosque and took literally centuries to complete. It contains much wonderful art, a lot of which is in the architecture. The pièce de résistance is the tomb of Christopher Columbus which is said to contain the remains of Columbus."

"Why do you say, 'said to contain'?" asked Ted.

"Well," said Katie, "the Dominican Republic claims that Columbus was buried there. But, in 2006, scientists ran DNA tests on samples from the five-hundred-year-old bones in the Seville tomb. From this test we know that at least some of Columbus' remains are there. It's known that Columbus' remains were moved several times after his death, and it's possible that some of the remains are in fact in the Dominican Republic. However, the director of the Columbus Lighthouse in Santo Domingo, where the alleged remains reside, has refused DNA samples. He says that 'Christian's don't bother the dead.' So we don't know all the facts as yet."

"Oh boy! I want to see Columbus' tomb. That's a cool thing I can tell my friends at school," exclaimed Teddy.

"Also," continued Katie, "next to the cathedral, is the *La Giralda*, a beautiful Moorish tower. It has somewhat become the symbol of Seville in pictures. You can climb to the top but there are no stairs, only what seems like an endless ramp which is wide enough for two horseman to ride up and down side by side. It's beautifully clear out today so the view from the top will be spectacular. Take a picture if you make it to the top, as there will be prizes for those who make it."

"Alright, more good candy?" asked Teddy.

"You'll see," said Katie, then continued. "We'll end our day at *Maria Luisa* Park. The park was dedicated to the sister of Isabella II and was the grounds of the *Palacio de San Telmo*. The royal park is now open to the public. The *River Guadalquivir* runs along the south side of the park, and you'll enjoy a horse and carriage ride along the river. Very relaxing and beautiful!"

"Hopefully your horse won't run off with you," joked Rick.

"I think I am going to pass on the horse and carriage ride," laughed Katie. "I'm not real trusting of animals right now. Dorothy, will you tell us a little about Bartolomé Esteban Murillo?"

"Sure," said Dorothy as she took Katie's place. "Murillo was born in 1617 and died in 1682 in the Sevilla area, and is therefore an artist of the Baroque period. He is best known for his religious works, but he also did paintings of flower girls, street urchins, and beggars which gives us an insightful look at everyday life during his time. He used his wife and baby daughter as subjects for two of his paintings, *The Virgin of the Rosary* and *Madonna and Child*. He lived most of his life in Seville, although he did spend a few years in Madrid. I think you will enjoy his beautiful art."

"Thanks, Dorothy. Well, it looks like we've arrived at the Alcázar," said Katie as the bus pulled up to a stop. "So let's go!"

They all enthusiastically got off the bus and started their day of touring. Late that afternoon the tired group arrived back at the hotel.

Agatha and Dorothy had made arrangements with Katie and Jorha to have dinner again in Katie's room, and they were going to go over all the information they could put together about the strange happenings. That evening, after another great takeout dinner, the group settled down to work.

"Those fresh fruit tarts are really good," commented Dorothy.

"You can say that again," agreed Agatha. "I'm glad we had a chance to have them a second time."

"Yes, Jorha and I usually get takeout in Seville. It's restful to stay in our rooms for a couple of nights, and the food is really good," said Katie.

"*Si, si,* so true," said Jorha, patting his stomach.

"Are you sure you ladies don't want to go out tonight?" asked Katie.

"No, it's good to rest, and we want to go over everything. This is a real mystery," said Agatha. "We need to find some answers."

"Well, I want you to know how much I appreciate you two," said Katie. "You have been someone to share my problems with, and Dorothy has been a big help speaking to the group."

"No problem," said Agatha.

"My pleasure," said Dorothy. "I enjoy doing it."

"Now, let's give Jake a call," said Agatha. "Jake is our next-door neighbor and a semi-retired police detective. He still does some consulting for the police department. I've known him for years because he use to make appearances all the time for the police in the criminal court where I worked. As I told you, Katie, I have been telling him about what has been happening on the trip and he has agreed to do a little research for us. I told him about this meeting and he wants to listen in and contribute if he can," said Agatha as she placed the call on her cell.

"Hola, Jake," she said as he answered the phone.

"Hi, Agatha," responded Jake.

"Jake, I have you on speaker phone so you can hear us, and we can hear you," explained Agatha. "Dorothy is here with Katie and Jorha."

"Hi, everyone," said Jake.

Everyone replied with a greeting.

"Now. Let's start by listing all the unusual things that have happened," suggested Agatha.

"Sounds good," said Katie pausing a moment to think. "Certainly the first strange thing that happened was Robbie's death on the plane," continued Katie. "I've had several tour members in the past get sick while on tour, and I've had two injured, but I have never had a tour member die, and there have been two deaths on this trip."

"Yes," said Agatha, "but let's don't get ahead of ourselves on the second one yet. I'm writing down, first strange occurrence, Robbie's death. It seems like it happened a long time ago, but it's really been just a little over a week. With all the red tape, his body just got back to the States yesterday. Is that right Jake?"

"Yes," said Jake. "There will be an autopsy and a toxicology report coming, but the autopsy alone will take another day or two. The toxicology report will take up to five days."

They all paused a moment to think about the delay.

"OK," continued Dorothy. "It will still be some time before we know if Robbie's death was the result of foul play. Let's see, the second thing that happened was the death of the poor little dog, Rolf."

"A dog!" said Jake.

"Yes," said Agatha, "and we wouldn't even include that incident, but Rolf died after licking up the spilt drink that Diane was supposed to drink. Did something in the drink kill him? We don't really know.

If it's found that Robbie died suspiciously, then maybe they should run tests on Rolf."

"Sounds reasonable," agreed Katie. "Can you make that happen Jake?"

"If we find out that Robbie did not die of natural causes, I will immediately be in contact with the police in Madrid," said Jake. "I know a detective there personally. Of course if there is a suspicion that Robbie was killed, all hell will break loose. You all would not be allowed to leave the country and continue your tour to Portugal for one thing because they wouldn't want you to leave their jurisdiction."

"Oh! I never thought of that," said Katie.

"Well, we don't have any information as yet. When do you cross into Portugal?" asked Jake. "It must be coming up soon."

"Yes, it is. We actually go into Portugal tomorrow," said Katie.

"Well you shouldn't be delayed then," said Jake. "It will be a while before we have any results."

"Whew! That's a relief," said Katie.

"Next, I think, is the rock in the windshield," continued Jorha.

"Yes, the rock that turned out to be a bullet," said Agatha. "I don't even know what to say about that, except it apparently came pretty close to you Katie."

"Yes, that's true," said Katie, "It was very scary."

"And it would have struck you had you been in your seat," shuddered Dorothy.

"True. Very scary. Again, it was chalked up as an accident," said Agatha. "Even after we discovered it was a bullet, the police thought it was a random shooting."

"Any of these things happening separately would not be so very strange in and of themselves," said Katie thoughtfully. "Of course

Robbie's death was tragic but it appeared to be from natural causes. I mean, he wasn't shot or stabbed or anything. It's just the cumulative effect of all that has happened that is so suspicious."

"True," said Agatha. "If someone is causing these things, they are pretty clever. Everything strange that has happened can be chalked up to accidents or normal occurrences."

"Yes, that is true. Okay, then we had the second death on the trip," said Dorothy.

"I can hardly bear to think about it," said Katie, as tears sprang into her eyes.

"I know," said Agatha. "Marian had been drinking pretty heavily that evening at the dinner. Did she fall and hit her head accidentally? And, if she didn't fall accidentally, why would anyone want to harm her?"

"*Señors* Rick and Dan, they were the last to see poor Marian," said Jorha.

"Yes, that's true, but Jake found no connection between them and Marian prior to the trip," said Dorothy.

"Right," said Jake. "But, I did learn that Rick and Dan are not who they say they are."

"What!" exclaimed Katie. "What do you mean?"

"Yes, I haven't told you that Jake found out that Rick and Dan are not brothers, and that they both live in Hollywood," said Agatha.

"So why would they tell the lie?" asked Jorha.

"That is a good question," said Jake, "but telling a lie doesn't necessarily mean they killed Marian, or anyone else. I haven't found any connection between them and anyone on the tour."

"Okay, now for a really bizarre happening," said Agatha. "The case of the runaway camel."

"That was odd, and at the time very frightening," exclaimed Katie.

"Did the man that stopped and talked to you send your camel off into the desert?" asked Agatha.

"I don't know," wondered Katie. "I didn't think so at the time but I guess he could have. His yelling seemed to make the camel go faster. I have no idea what he was saying."

"I don't want to scare you more, but if those Brits had not come by, you could have died out there," said Agatha. "That's twice on this trip that you were at risk of being killed."

"I know," agreed Katie. "Believe me, I have had nightmares about it. But why would anyone want to kill me. I don't have any enemies that I know of."

"I don't know," said Agatha shaking her head. "Now, what have we learned from Jake and from our observations? First occurrence, Robbie's death."

"We will know a lot more after the autopsy and tests," said Dorothy.

"Yes, but we do have a little information. Remember Jake found out that Robbie came from Troy, Ohio, just like the Dave and Diane," said Agatha.

"Hmm! So chances are they would have known each other as they appeared to be about the same age, and Troy's a very small town. They just didn't get the chance to meet up on the tour," said Katie.

"And Dotty, do you remember who didn't go to sleep on the plane?" asked Agatha.

"Oh dear Lord, I do," answered Dorothy. "Dave. Do you think that means anything?"

"Dave?" asked Katie.

"Yes, he said he stayed awake while the rest of us napped," remembered Dorothy. "And, Diane had taken something to sleep. We were asleep too. We don't know what Dave did during that time. But Dave's too nice to do anything bad."

"Well, in my years in the criminal court, I have seen many people who appear nice, but who have done bad things," said Agatha.

"I'll say amen to that," commented Jake. "If criminals all had a certain personality it would be a lot easier to find them."

"Well, Jessica was sitting with Robbie," said Dorothy. "Look at my sketch book."

Everyone looked at the sketch Dorothy had done of the inside of the plane with the passengers seated. Robbie and Jessica were recognizable sitting toward the back of the plane.

"But that was early in the flight," said Agatha. "She soon moved away from him."

"That's true," said Katie. "They were sitting together the first time I checked on the tour group but not thereafter, and I saw Robbie alive after she had moved."

"Of course, most of us were asleep or dozing," said Agatha, "so anyone could have gone back to Robbie."

"True," agreed Dorothy. "I know I was out like a light."

"But Dave wasn't," reiterated Katie.

"No, Dave wasn't," agreed Agatha. "There may have been others on the tour who were not asleep also. We don't know."

"Unfortunately I was dozing during that time also," said Katie.

"OK, let's move on to the second incident," said Agatha. "Poor little Rolf."

"Well, we know the drink was intended for Diane," said Dorothy. "You and I were standing there when the waiter brought it to her. I think he said it was from Dave."

"No," said Agatha thinking hard. "I think Diane assumed it was from Dave."

"Hmm, you may be right," said Dorothy thoughtfully.

"It could have been from Dave," said Katie.

"But if Diane had been the one to drink it, would she have been sick, or worse yet, would she have died?" asked Dorothy. "There may have been nothing in the drink, and Rolf just died of something else."

"We have no way of knowing, yet," said Agatha. "Hopefully if Robbie's death turns out to be suspicious we can find out. Well, let's go on. What about the bullet, Jorha? Neither Dorothy nor I were on the bus when that happened."

"Very bad, very bad," said Jorha. "We thought it was the rock. It made very loud noise when it hit the window."

"It must have just missed me," Katie said with frightened eyes. "We never dreamed, however, that it was a bullet at the time. Did we Jorha?"

"No. It was *señorita* Agatha who found the bullet," said Jorha. "I believe she dug it from the seat."

"I'm too curious for my own good," said Agatha.

"But in this case, curiosity was good," put in Jake. "The police have the bullet but haven't connected it with anything in their systems."

"Another dead end. Sorry about digging around in your seat," said Agatha to Katie. "I was careful not to make the hole any bigger."

"No problem," said Katie shaking her head. "It's not my van, and it's a good thing that you dug it out or we might never have known that the rock was really a bullet. Hmm, let's see, I guess Marian is next. Right?"

"Yes," said Dorothy. "Have you learned anything more, Jake?"

"No," responded Jake. "I cannot find any connection between Marian and anyone else on the tour. She seems to be exactly who she said she was, Marian the Librarian."

"I've been wondering if the fact that Marian was wearing Diane's shawl could be significant," said Agatha. "Remember she borrowed it from Diane."

"You're right! Do you think someone thought it was Diane instead of Marian?" asked Dorothy.

"Well, if there was something in the spilt drink targeting Diane, it would be more consistent than someone murdering Marian," said Agatha.

The group was silent for a moment. No one before had said the word murder out loud, even though that had obviously been on their minds.

"Murder! Such an ugly word," said Katie softly. "Dear Lord! How could this be happening?"

"Well, don't jump to conclusions yet," said Jake. "We don't know for sure that anyone has been murdered at this point. However, I want you all to be very careful and very watchful."

"Judge Smith would always say that there was no such thing as a coincidence when it came to crime. Should we tell Diane anything?" asked Agatha.

"No, I don't think so, yet," said Jake. "Although it appears that Diane and Katie could be targets. All of you should keep an eye on them, but I don't think there is any reason to upset Diane at this point."

"Why would I be a target?" said Katie. "I have no enemies that I know of, and why me and Diane? I've never met her before that I can remember, and I bet she would say she has never met me. This is all crazy."

"I will protect *señorita* Katie," said Jorha. "No more camels will run with her."

"Good," said Jake.

"I can take care of myself," said Katie looking at Jorha appreciatively. "But, we must all watch over Diane."

"We will do that," agreed Agatha. "I don't want to sound melodramatic, but I feel there is evil lurking somewhere in this group."

# TRAVEL TIPS FROM AGATHA AND DOROTHY

*The best bullfighters in Spain appear from Easter until late summer at the *Maestranza* bullring on Paseo de Cristóbal Colón (tel. 95-450-13-82). The bullfights are usually on Sunday. Tickets are expensive and should be purchased in advance at the ticket office on *Calle Adriano*. There are many ticket kiosks on the main shopping street, *Calle Sierpes*, but these charge a 20% or more commission. There are movements to make bullfighting illegal. It is already illegal in the Catalonia area of Spain. So, if you go to Barcelona, you will not be going to a bullfight.

**Shorts and T-shirts are not allowed in the cathedral. You will be turned away if not dressed properly.

# CHAPTER 11

*Day 11*

---

Seville—Lisbon: We cross the border into the maritime
Algarve area of Portugal. This province is called the
Garden of Portugal and includes a coastline of almost
one hundred miles. We will have lunch near Lagos on
the coast. Our ultimate destination is Lisbon, Portugal's
capital city.

---

"Good morning," said Katie as she boarded the bus enthusiastically. "We have an exciting day and a very picturesque drive ahead of us. We're leaving Spain for a couple of days and crossing over into Portugal. Personally, I love Portugal. It's one of my most favorite countries, and it's one that is not on a lot of Americans' itineraries. Portugal is more of what we generally, in our imaginations, think traditional Europe should be. In the Portuguese countryside, the people remain living a more traditional lifestyle. You'll see women carrying loads of various kinds on their heads, oxen pulling carts, and fishermen with their brightly painted fishing boats pulled up onto the shore. Unfortunately, you'll also see many fishermen's widows dressed in black, who live on very small government pensions. All part of life in the seafaring country of Portugal. This morning we will drive to Lagos, where we'll stop for lunch. Then this afternoon, we'll drive on to Lisbon."

"As we drive through this area," Katie continued, "notice the many castles and fortresses on distant hilltops. We'll also be traveling close to the shore, where you can enjoy beautiful vistas of beaches along the Atlantic Ocean. We'll have lunch at Rouxinol,* a restaurant that is about twenty-six miles outside the seaside town of Lagos. It has an outstanding chef, who is also the owner. I would suggest ordering the shellfish stew or the freshly caught fish of the day. However, if you do not want seafood, the grilled lamb is also excellent. For dessert try the warm raspberry pie with ice cream. We called ahead, and it's on the menu today. Yum! I can hardly wait for lunch, their food is so good."

"I'll tell you about Lisbon and our hotel this afternoon," said Katie. "But for now, just enjoy the ride. The scenery is beautiful, you can read, or those of us who are knitting can work on our scarves. Who knows? In three hours, I should be able to get—oh, I don't know—maybe two whole rows done."

"Very funny," said Agatha. "With twenty stitches per row, you should get a lot more than that done. I'll come around and help anyone who needs it."

"That would be me," said Lora. "You said twenty stitches? How come I have twenty-two?"

"Hmm! And I have nineteen stitches," said Nancy looking puzzled.

"Coming to help," laughed Agatha as she left her seat and went back toward Lora and Nancy, who were sitting together near the rear of the bus.

"I would like you to check my knitting, too," said Chelsie as Agatha passed her seat.

"Will do," said Agatha. "I'll be right back."

"Okay, what do we have?" asked Agatha as she took the seat across the aisle from Lora.

Lora handed Agatha her lovely, soft teal-blue yarn and her knitting needles.

"Just what I suspected," said Agatha. "When you finish a row, you need to be sure the yarn is straight. Do you see how, if the yarn is on the wrong side, it looks like two stitches? See, if it's on the right side it looks like one stitch."

"Wow!" you're right exclaimed Lora.

"If you knit the two instead of one, you will add a stitch at the end of each row. That's one reason I suggested you count your stitches when you finish each row until you're more confident. Even then, you still should count stitches about every five rows or so. Counting just limits the amount you have to take out if there is a mistake. Unraveling stitches is called frogging."

"Frogging!" exclaimed Lora. "That's a funny name."

"It is, and I have no idea why it's called frogging, but beginning knitters become very familiar with frogging. However, even very experienced knitters have to frog once in a while. You want your knitting to be as perfect as possible, so you have to correct mistakes as you go along."

"Change seats with me, Lora," said Nancy, "so Agatha can see what I did wrong."

"Okay, here you go," agreed Lora getting up.

Once Nancy was settled, she handed her knitting to Agatha.

"Hmm," said Agatha as she looked carefully at Nancy's knitting. "It looks like you dropped a stitch a couple of rows back. Look, you can see it." Agatha laid the knitting flat on her lap. The lime-green yarn contrasted well with Agatha's black plants, and the dropped stitch was obvious.

"Oh dear," exclaimed Nancy with a big frown on her face. "What do I do now?"

"Well, you need to do some frogging also," laughed Agatha, "but it's not that serious. You can pull out the needle and pull on the yarn to take out the two rows, and then carefully pick up the stitches with your needle. Or you can do it one stitch at a time, leaving the stitches on the one needle and using your other knitting needle to take off one stitch at a time, or you can kind of weave the dropped stitch up the two rows. Let me show you how to do it the second way, one stitch at a time. That is the safest when you are learning. You may want to watch this, Lora. You might need it sometime."

"If it's something used to correct a mistake, I'm sure I will," laughed Lora.

Agatha carefully worked her way back to the dropped stitch, picked it up, and re-knitted the two rows she had taken out for Nancy.

"There you go, Nancy," said Agatha, handing the knitting back to her. "Right back where you were. The other knitters are a little ahead of you, so they already have had the frogging lesson."

"You can say that again," giggled Diane, who was sitting a row in front of Lora and Nancy. "I am a frogging expert."

"I've got to go show this to Rubio," said Nancy as she gathered her knitting together and stood up. "He'll be so proud of me."

Agatha moved over into her vacated seat.

"Are you enjoying the trip?" asked Agatha, looking intently at Lora.

"Of course," said Lora. "Spain is such a beautiful country."

"You've missed so much of the touring by visiting Rubio's relatives," commented Agatha.

"True," said Lora dropping her eyes to her knitting.

"Isn't that disappointing?" asked Agatha. "I know I would hate being in these beautiful countries and not seeing many of the sights."

Lora was silent a minute and finally leaned close to Agatha and whispered, "Can you keep a secret?"

"Definitely," said Agatha.

"Well, we're not really visiting relatives. We're looking for sites to open new yogurt stores. We have quite a few shops in the United States, and now we're expanding to Spain," confided Lora.

"Oh," said Agatha and let this information sink in.

"Why take a tour to do it, and why keep it a secret?" asked Agatha

"When we went to the tour office, we were going to tour independently, but this group was going where we wanted to go, and going on a tour, relieved us of taking care of details like hotels, transportation, fooling with our luggage, etc.," explained Lora. "None of us like to do that sort of thing."

"But why keep it a secret?" asked Agatha again.

"Because we have competitors who always want to know what we're doing," said Lora. "Our business is very successful, and we have a lot of copycats. They don't know we are expanding to Europe and certainly not where in Europe."

"Okay, sounds reasonable. Why Spain for your first expansion?" asked Agatha curiously.

"Actually, we are looking at Spain and Italy. We obviously do better in warm weather selling frozen yogurt," explained Lora. "Oh-oh! Here comes Nancy. I'm not supposed to be talking about this to anyone. Please don't tell."

"No problem!" said Agatha. "My lips are sealed."

Agatha stood up to make room for Nancy and went to where Chelsie sat with Stanley.

"Hey! You are making great progress, Chelsie," said Agatha as she stood in the aisle and watched Chelsie knit. "You have a real knack for knitting."

"Thanks," said Chelsie. "I think I'm okay, but I just wanted you to double-check."

"It's beautiful," appraised Agatha picking up the scarf and looking closely at the stitches. "I love the purple. Such a pretty color. Your stitches are very even and not too tight nor too loose. That is very hard to do for a newbie. Congratulations! What do you think, Stanley? Isn't it pretty?"

"Yeah!" said Stanley. "Only she should have gotten brown yarn so she could make one for me."

"Oh, right!" said Chelsie as she punched Stanley on the arm. "Seriously though! I will make one for you if you want me too."

"Cool!" said Stanley. "Can you do it before we finish the trip?"

"No, I don't think so," answered Chelsie.

"I don't know. You're making pretty good time," commented Agatha. "I think you could finish this one today, if you really work at it, depending how long you want it to be, of course."

"Yeah, maybe," said Chelsie. "Okay, Stanley. You can buy some yarn in Lisbon, and I will knit it for you."

"That's a deal. Thanks!" said Stanley with a big smile.

"How's your mother doing with her knitting?" asked Agatha as she looked at the seat behind Chelsie in which Linda was sitting.

"I'm doing pretty good," smiled Linda. "Just not as well as Chelsie."

Linda handed her knitting to Agatha to check.

"You're right! This looks very good," said Agatha. "Good job! Knitting talent must run in the family!"

While Agatha was checking the knitting, Dorothy had sauntered back to where Marian usually sat, in front of Rick and Dan.

"Hi, guys," said Dorothy as she flopped down and turned around. "How are you two doing?"

"We're good," said Dan smiling. "And how are you and Agatha?"

"We're good, too," said Dorothy. "Are you enjoying the tour, in spite of Marian's terrible accident?"

"You know, this is really an outstanding tour," said Dan. "It's terrible what happened to Marian, but we decided we couldn't dwell on it since there is nothing we can do about it now. I just wish we had stayed with her at the time."

"I know," sympathized Dorothy, "but it wasn't your fault at all. You had no way of knowing something would happen to her. No one would have anticipated such a thing."

"Yes, well that's why we are trying not to worry about it," said Rick.

"Agatha and I were wondering, were other people out and around when you went back to your room?" asked Dorothy.

"A few. Mostly hotel staff, I think," said Dan.

"Did you see any of our group?" continued Dorothy.

"No, I don't think so. Why?" asked Rick.

"I don't know. No real reason," replied Dorothy. "Agatha and I keep thinking about it and trying to figure it out. It was just so bizarre. Oh, by the way, I've been meaning to ask you. My cousin is moving to Chicago soon and is trying to figure out where to look for housing. Where would you suggest, Rick?"

"Gee, it's been a long time since I . . . ," started Rick.

Everyone was quiet for a minute as Dorothy looked from Rick to Dan and then back to Rick.

"Actually," said Rick looking guilty, "although I, um, I consider myself from Chicago, I haven't lived there for a while."

"Oh! Where do you live?" asked Dorothy innocently.

Both Rick and Dan were silent again. They looked at each and nodded.

"Dorothy, can you keep a confidence?" asked Dan turning back to Dorothy.

"Yes, of course," responded Dorothy.

"You live in California, right?" asked Dan.

"Yes!"

"Then you know what domestic partners are," said Dan. "Rick and I are domestic partners. Have been since before gay marriage was legal."

"Oh! But why did you say you were brothers?" questioned Dorothy puzzled.

"You're familiar with domestic partners, being from California, but a lot of people aren't. When we travel, we keep our personal life, well, personal," explained Rick. "It just makes things easier."

"Oh, I'm sorry I got nosy," said Dorothy. "I certainly will not spread it around. It's no one's business, including mine."

"That's okay," said Rick. "We wouldn't have told you if we didn't think you and Agatha would be cool about it. I assume you'll mention it to Agatha."

"Yeah, probably, if it's okay, and thank you," said Dorothy. "I take it as a compliment that you feel that way about us, even though we're old!"

"Very funny," laughed Dan. "You two are not old. Old isn't age; it's attitude. You two have young souls. Actually, we thought maybe you two were. . . "

"Oh! No! We have been friends since we were five. Agatha was married and has several children. What you said about us having young souls is sweet. Thank you," exclaimed Dorothy smiling broadly. "And thanks for satisfying my curiosity, as inappropriate as it was."

"No problem," said Rick.

It was soon lunchtime, and everyone was hungry as the bus pulled to a stop in front of the restaurant. Katie had been right about the chef. The food was excellent, especially the dessert. After lunch they all climbed back on the bus for the final leg of the journey to Lisbon.

Katie assumed her usual position and said, "We will be in Lisbon in about three hours, depending on the traffic. Lisbon is the Portuguese capital. What is particularly nice about Portugal is that the sights are not overrun by tourists, at least compared with other European countries. Lisbon is actually one of the oldest cities in the world, predating London, Paris, and Rome by hundreds of years. We will be staying at the York House Hotel.** It was once a seventeenth-century Carmelite convent just outside the center of Lisbon. Dorothy, you will be happy to know that it's near the National Ancient Art Gallery. The gallery is less than a mile away from the hotel. It's a wonderful museum, and you should have time to run over there when we arrive at our hotel, assuming we don't hit bad traffic. It's certainly worth seeing for all of you."

"Wonderful, thank you," said Dorothy.

"The hotel we're staying in has an award-winning restaurant featuring French-Portuguese cuisine." continued Katie. "However, when I am in Portugal I love to eat a simple meal of soup and bread. They are so good, I can never get enough of them; so be sure to order soup with your dinner. You won't regret it. One of the hotel's best features is its staff. Very friendly and helpful, and most speak English and French, along with Portuguese. The hotel is located on a hillside overlooking the Tagus River and has lovely gardens. I think you'll be very comfortable there. This will be a rest day for you to prepare for the next two days which will entail a lot of walking. So, rest up! Are there any questions?"

"If we don't want to go to the art gallery, what's a good alternative?" asked Rubio.

"A ride on Tram 28 would be fun," answered Katie. "I'll show you where to catch it. It runs until 11:00 p.m., but if you get stuck somewhere, just jump into a taxi. They're very reasonably priced. I'll give you the usual "How to Get Back to the Hotel" card. The tram runs through several historic districts, along cobbled streets. By the way, in general, Lisbon is a safe city, but on the tram watch out for pickpockets. Keep valuables tucked away in a safe place. Now if you prefer to shop, head for *Amoreiras* Shopping Center. The center has more than two hundred and fifty shops. Or, you can try *Centro Colombo*, the largest shopping center on the Iberian Peninsula, which has more than four hundred shops. You will find plenty of places to eat there, if you wish. *Centro Colombo* has more than sixty restaurants, but remember that the restaurant in our hotel is outstanding."

"Which shopping center is the closest?" asked Nancy.

"The *Amoreiras*," answered Katie, "and since time will be limited, I would go there instead of *Colombo*."

"Are there any more questions?" asked Katie as she looked around at the group. "Good!Seeing none, I will get back to my knitting. Enjoy the ride."

The afternoon trip was pleasant and uneventful. They arrived in less than three hours, so Agatha and Dorothy had plenty of time to go to the museum after checking into their room.

As Katie had promised it was a wonderful museum, holding Portugal's greatest collection of paintings, in a lovely seventeenth-century palace. Most memorable was the polyptych* from St. Vincent's monastery, thought to have been done by Nuno Gonçalves in the fifteenth century. The six panels that comprise the polyptych were amazing. They featured Henry the Navigator, the Portuguese sailor who explored the unknown sea, although there are sixty persons in the panels representing several social groups of fifteenth century Portugal. Dorothy and Agatha wished they had more time to view the collection at leisure, and thought that, perhaps, one day they would come back.

After returning to the hotel, the ladies had a delicious late dinner, and then went up to their room.

As they were unlocking the door, Agatha's phone rang.

After checking who was calling, she answered, "Hi, Jake!" Who else could it be?

"Hi, Agatha," responded Jake. "Are you where you can talk for a minute?"

"Oh yes," said Agatha. "We just got back to our room."

"Good! You better sit down because I have some startling news for you.

"Oh no! What?" said Agatha

"It has been confirmed that Robbie's death was the result of foul play."

# TRAVEL TIPS FROM AGATHA AND DOROTHY

*Rouxinol, Estrada de Monchique*, tel. (28/291-39-75). This restaurant is closed in December and January. The restaurant has some of the best regional cuisine in the area. It's in an old hunting lodge. One of Agatha and Dorothy's favorites.

**York House Hotel, *Rua das Janelas Verdes* 32, 1200-691 *Lisboa*, tel. (21/396-24-35). This hotel is outside busy Lisbon, and gives the traveler some peace and tranquility. Its location is on a hillside overlooking the Tagus River.

# CHAPTER 12

*Day 12*

---

*Lisbon and Sintra: An early-morning trip to the fairy-tale world of Sintra, where we will visit Palácio Nacional da Pena, Castelo dos Mouros, and Palácio Nacional de Sintra. After lunch, we journey back to Lisbon by way of Belém.*

---

It was official. Robbie had not died of natural causes. It appeared he had been poisoned, but they would have to wait for the toxicology report to be sure. Jake also said that the police in Madrid had been notified, and that the tour group would be questioned when they returned to Spain. Robbie had died on the plane. The tour group had not formed at that time, so there were hundreds of suspects, that is, all of the passengers on the plane. Jake had said that he still had some convincing to do before the authorities would dig up Rolf's remains. He thought he could convince them to do it because if the dog had died of the same poison that Robbie died from, it could limit the suspects for his murder to the tour group. Jake also asked that only Katie be told anything about the coming police investigation because he did not want to give any potential murderer notice that he or she would be questioned once they returned to Madrid. Agatha had immediately called Katie to tell her. Katie had been shocked but not exceptionally surprised.

The group met very early to start a full touring day. Once all the sleepy travelers were settled on the bus, Katie began her explanation of the day ahead of them.

"Good morning," said Katie, not quite as bouncy and upbeat as usual. "We will start our day by visiting beautiful *Sintra*, which is located just eighteen miles outside Lisbon. *Sintra* is a fairy-tale town which Lord Byron called a 'glorious eden'. Some who visit *Sintra* cannot bear to leave and they stay forever; so be careful," smiled Katie.

"In *Sintra*, we will first visit the *Palácio Nacional da Pena*. The Pena is known as a castle in the sky, located high above Sintra. Part of the fun of visiting it is the ride up on a winding road through the *Parque das Merendas*. It is so very beautiful! From the top, you will have a vista clear to the outskirts of Lisbon. The castle was built in the early nineteenth century by King-consort Ferdinand II of Austria, who was married to Maria II. He wanted to build a fantasy castle, and the castle looks like something that could be part of Walt Disney's Fantasyland. Ferdinand wanted a castle built to rival the beautiful Neuschwanstein Castle in Bavaria. He asked Baron Wilhelm Ludwig von Eschwege to create the castle, and the only input he gave the Baron was that he wanted it to reflect an opera. Whatever that meant! He didn't even say which opera. The exterior is very colorful, much of it being candy-colored yellow and pink. You should also notice the mythological characters around the windows and the grotesque gargoyles looking down on you as you go through the main entrance. King Ferdinand loved the castle and spent most of his last years there."

"The interior is much as Queen Amelia left it in 1910," continued Katie, "when she realized that the monarchy in Portugal was ending. Her husband and one of her sons had been assassinated, and she was afraid for her second son, Manuel II. The castle is a superb record of how the European royals lived in the days preceding the First World War."

"From Pena we will go into the town of *Sintra* and see *Palacio Nacional de Sintra*, which is just outside the town center. This too was a royal palace until 1910 and is where Queen Maria Pia, the Italian grandmother of Manuel II, the last king of Portugal, lived. The castle is built on the property where a summer palace for Moorish sultans was previously located. In 1863, that palace was completely razed to make room for a new castle. Moorish-style architecture was incorporated into the new version. Be sure to go up to the castle's turrets and view the oversized conical chimney towers for the kitchen. They are unique. Also, the glazed earthenware tiles in some of the rooms are among the most beautiful in Portugal. When you're finished viewing the castle, walk back into *Sintra* and have an early lunch, which should be fine since you had such an early breakfast. You may want to wait to shop until tomorrow, when we will stop at a fete where we have a local who will help you get a good price on hand-embroidered linens and hand-painted ceramics. Okay," said Katie looking out the front window of the bus, "we are almost there. Enjoy your day!"

*Sintra* was all that Katie said it would be, and more. Agatha and Dorothy agreed that they would like to return to Sintra. It's such a beautiful spot in this big world. They returned to the bus after an excellent lunch at a small restaurant just off the main square. They especially loved the soup and delicious bread; Katie was right. They were ready now for a busy afternoon.

Again all were settled on the bus, and Jorha started back to Lisbon by way of Belém.

"I trust you all enjoyed *Sintra*," said Katie as she began her spiel about their afternoon. "It truly is a wonderful place."

Everyone on the bus agreed, and Linda said that there was something truly magical about the area.

"So many people feel that," said Katie. "But I know you will enjoy the rest of the day too. Our next stop will be Belém, located where the Tagus River meets the sea. It's the spot from which the great Portuguese explorers set out: Vasco da Gama to India, Ferdinand Magellan to sail around the globe, and Bartolomeu Dias to round the Cape of Good Hope. This area became very rich, especially as spices began to pour into the port. Our first stop will be *Torre de Belém,* or Tower of Belém, which is right on the shore. *Torre de Belém* is on the waterline, and you can sit on the steps and listen to the water lap against them. The tower looks like a small castle in the Manueline style, blending Gothic and Moorish elements. It was actually built in 1515 as a fortress to guard the city. In 1580, it became a prison under Spanish control. It held political prisoners for more than fifty years but later became a customs house. From the tower we will walk over to *Padrão dos Descobrimentos.* I love this monument. It's in the shape of the prow of a *caravela,* a type of ship used by explorers during the fifteenth and sixteenth centuries. Up a ramp on each side of the prow are figures made of stone representing several explorers as well as royalty, mathematicians, writers, artists, monks, cartographers, and cosmographers. Where the two ramps meet is a figure representing Henry the Navigator, who opened up new worlds as he sailed into what was then called the Sea of Darkness. This monument is relatively new, for Portugal, having been unveiled in 1960. On the ground in front of the monument is a map of the world with dates of Portuguese discoveries set in metal. We actually owe the Portuguese a great deal for their brave explorations."

"What are, uh, whatever the two 'c' or maybe 'k' words were?" asked Teddy.

"'C' or 'k' words? Oh—'c' words," said Katie after thinking a minute. "Cartographers and cosmographers?"

"Yeah, those words," confirmed Teddy.

"I know what a cartographer is," said Dave. "A mapmaker, but I don't know what a cosmographer is. Something to do with the cosmos. Hmm, come to think of it, I don't exactly know what the cosmos is. Maybe the universe?"

"Yes, pretty much. A cosmographer studies geography and astronomy. Cartographers and cosmographers were necessary for the exploration of the world," said Katie.

"Anyway, continuing with our day, from the *Padrão dos Descobrimentos* we will get back on the bus for the short ride to the monastery, *Mosteiro dos Jerónimos*. Manuel I, the Fortunate, had this monastery built to commemorate Vasco da Gama's voyage to India and to give thanks for the success of the trip. It too is in the Manueline style with Gothic and Moorish influences. We will enter the south portal, where there are elaborate carvings of the Virgin of Belém. Belém means Bethlehem, by the way. The west door of the church leads to the cloisters, where the stone sculpture is incredibly intricate. Vasco da Gama is entombed at the monastery, as is the author, Luis Vaz de Camões. Both tombs rest on the backs of lions. You will enjoy the visit to the monastery, but the real reason I include it on the tour is so we can stop by *Pastéis de Belém** to get custard cream tarts. They are like nothing you have tasted, they are so unbelievably good. When the monasteries closed around 1834, the monks needed to make a living and they began selling the tarts. The tarts became so popular that people would come all the way from Lisbon just to buy them. The recipe is a long-held secret and has been passed down in its original form. Yum!"

"Sounds good to me," commented Rick. "I'm full right now, but by then I should be ready for a snack."

"Me, too," agreed Dan.

"Okay," said Katie. "Everyone out of the bus for our Belém sights."

Two hours later the tour group members were munching their custard tarts as they rode on to Lisbon proper.

"How are the tarts?" Katie asked.

Everyone responded in the affirmative, especially Teddy.

"They are wonderful," said Agatha, "but I couldn't talk them out of the recipe. I'll have to try to figure it out at home."

"No, I'm sure you could not! The recipe is a long-kept secret. Okay, on to Lisbon," said Katie.

"We will start our tour of Lisbon by driving around the *Praça do Comércio* which is the neoclassical square facing the Tagus River. Our first stop will be at the twelfth-century *Sé* Cathedral. It was built on the site of an old mosque. We'll have a guide take us through the sacristy and cloister, which I think you will find interesting. Portugal's nobility and elite were baptized, married, and buried at the cathedral. From there we will go to *Castelo de São Jorge*. This castle was built by the Moors in the tenth century, and it then served as a royal palace from the thirteenth to the sixteenth centuries. It fell into great disrepair, and little of the original structure remains. A twentieth-century reconstruction was undertaken to evoke some of the original grandeur. Walk the esplanades and climb the ramparts of the old castle for incredible views of the Tagus and the old Alfama district. The locals believe this district to be the birthplace of Lisbon. Candy for all who make the climb."

"That will be me! What's an esplanade?" asked Teddy.

"It's an open area, often a promenade, where people may walk, along a river," replied Katie. "Our tour for the day will end at the *Museu Nacional dos Coches,* the National Coach Museum. Believe it or not, this is the most visited attraction in Lisbon. It's the best museum of its type in the world. The museum is located in a former eighteenth-century riding academy, and the coaches stand in a former horse ring. Most of the coaches date from the seventeenth to the nineteenth centuries."

"That will be the last stop on our tour today," continued Katie. "I know it has been a long day, and I hope you have enjoyed it. After the museum, we will take you back to the hotel, or you can strike out on your own for dinner if you like."

"Do we have to decide right now?" asked Nancy.

"No, not at all," replied Katie. "Just tell us before we leave the museum so we don't hold the bus for you."

The rest of the afternoon went well and was most enjoyable. Lisbon is a beautiful city, and the people are very friendly. With the exception of Rick and Dan, all of the travelers returned to the hotel because they were quite tired after their busy day.

Agatha and Dorothy longed to get to their room and lay down for a little while. Their feet hurt! After a half-hour nap, they decided to eat at the hotel restaurant. They were seated in a booth that had very high backs and sides, which gave them an intimate feel. All they needed was a couple of cool guys. Oh well! Maybe the next trip. Agatha and Dorothy could not even see who was seated around them. They both ordered the local specialty, recommended by the waiter, *bacalhau com natas,* which turned out to be salted cod, onions, and potatoes with cream. The waiter told them it was spiced with nutmeg and white pepper. Most delicious!

The two tired travelers were lingering over a cup of herb tea when they heard Katie talking about *Sintra* in the booth behind them.

"I'll ask Katie if she wants us to come up to her room," said Agatha.

"Good idea," said Dorothy.

Agatha got up and walked around to the booth behind them.

"Katie, do you want to meet in your room to discuss. . ." Agatha stopped dead in her tracks as she peered into the booth and realized that the voice she had heard had not been Katie's but Jessica.

"Jessica! I'm—I'm sorry! I thought you were Katie. Uh, hi, Diane, Dave," said Agatha, stuttering a little.

The three seated in the booth looked up and greeted Agatha.

"Why would you want to meet in Katie's room?" asked Dave frowning. "What are you discussing?"

"Uh, well, uh, Katie got her knitting into a mess, and she asked me to help her straighten it out," replied Agatha, thinking fast. Of all people to slip up with—Dave. Right now, our number-one suspect. "We were just talking about *Sintra*," said Diane. "We loved that area, didn't you?"

"We did," said Agatha.

"Me, too," said Dorothy from the next booth as she slid out and joined everyone.

"Dorothy, do you want to join us while Agatha helps Katie with her knitting?" asked Dave.

"No," said Dorothy quickly. "I—uh—I'm tired and need to turn in early, but thanks!"

"I don't blame you," said Diane, "I'm tired, too. I think we will all sleep well tonight."

They all said their goodnights, and Agatha and Dorothy went up to their room.

"Whew!" said Agatha.

"Yeah!" said Dorothy. "I'm getting better at lying! I'm not sure that's a good thing."

"You are getting better. Sorry about that," said Agatha grinning. "Did you notice that Dave was really interested in what we were discussing with Katie?"

"Yes, but I still can't believe Dave is a bad guy," said Dorothy.

"I know. I like him, too," agreed Agatha, "and I can't believe he would want to harm Diane. They seem a devoted couple. Well, we get back to Spain tomorrow. It all hits the fan, and we'll see how everyone reacts to the news of Robbie's death and to being questioned by the police."

"Do you think we will be questioned?" asked Dorothy.

"Are you kidding? I'm sure we will," said Agatha. "We were among the last people to see Robbie alive."

"I've been thinking," said Dorothy. "Do you think Robbie committed suicide?"

"If he did, then we are back to having all of these weird occurrences being unconnected, and that seems doubtful. And why would someone commit suicide on a plane on the way to a trip of a lifetime? That seems really unlikely."

When the two ladies returned to their room, they immediately got ready for bed. They would not be leaving as early the next day as they had that morning, but they wanted to get a good night's sleep. They knew the next couple of days would be difficult. After all, it appeared that they really did have a murderer in their midst.

# TRAVEL TIPS FROM AGATHA AND DOROTHY

*If you are in Belém, be sure to stop by Pastéis de Belém at Rua de Belém 84. When the monasteries closed in 1834, the clergy started selling these pastries to earn money for food. The tarts became very popular with visitors. The recipe remains unchanged since 1834, and has been passed down for almost two hundred years. They are made in a "secret room," and not even Agatha could talk them out of the recipe. Sorry?

# CHAPTER 13

## Day 13

---

*Lisbon—Fatíma—Salamanca: We travel north through the picturesque Sierra de Aire on our way to the Shrine at Fatíma to visit the Basilica of Our Lady of the Rosary. We then return to Spain and on to Salamanca to view the Baroque Plaza Mayor, one of Spain's grandest squares.*

---

"Stop," yelled Dorothy as she sat up in bed.

"What's wrong, Dotty," said Agatha sleepily raising up on one arm. "Are you OK? What happened?"

Dorothy looked at Agatha, somewhat confused. "I must have had a nightmare," said Dorothy in a small voice.

Agatha got out of bed and sat down on the side of Dorothy's bed. "I'm sorry! I didn't know you had nightmares," she said. "Are you okay?"

"I'm fine," replied Dorothy. "I rarely have a nightmare. I haven't had one in years, so I wasn't expecting it. I'm so sorry I woke you up. What time is it?"

"It's a little after seven. We need to be getting up anyway. What was your dream about?"

"It seems silly now, but boy was it real while I was asleep," said Dorothy waking up a little more. "I dreamt that we were on the bus and approaching the Spanish border and there were a bunch of police cars lined up facing us across the road with their lights blinking red, and instead of stopping, Jorha blew right through them and the police started chasing us. Jorha was laughing hysterically and Katie was urging him on. The rest of us were screaming. Then we went over a hill, and as we reached the top we could see this big truck heading right for us. That's when I screamed, 'Stop' and then woke up. My heart is still pounding."

"Nightmares can seems so real," sympathized Agatha.

They both got dressed, had breakfast, and loaded onto the bus, ready for whatever the day had in store for them. The weather was beautiful, which lifted the spirits of all the travelers, though they were tired after almost two weeks of being on the go. Of course, the group at large did not know what was in store for them when they returned to Madrid. Agatha and Dorothy knew that they would all be questioned by the police before they could go home. Not a pleasant way to end a trip.

The group was due to fly home in two days, and the police would need strong evidence to hold any of them, let alone all of them. No, they wouldn't hold all of them, would they? This isn't an "Orient Express" murder with multiple culprits.* At least Agatha didn't think so.

"Good morning," said Katie, looking as cheerful as she could under the circumstances. Today we head back to Spain, with first a last stop in Portugal at the world-famous pilgrimage site, *Fatíma*. Many people, especially the Portuguese, go on a pilgrimage to *Fatíma* to pay for their sins. As penance, people crawl across the square, which is twice as big as the Vatican Square, on their knees. A long walkway of marble has been built to make it a little easier, but it's still got to hurt. Marble is smooth but it's a very hard surface. There is almost always someone painfully sliding along the walkway."

It went through Agatha's mind that there was likely someone in the group who could use sin forgiveness—big time.

"So why do people go to *Fatíma* as a pilgrimage?" asked Rick.

"Because on May 13, 1917, the Virgin Mary reputedly appeared to three shepherd children. The children said that a year before she appeared to them, they saw an angel of peace to prepare them for her coming. The Virgin Mary is said to have appeared to the children six times, between May and October of 1917. She reportedly told the children three secrets, one about the coming of World Wars, one about the rejection of God by Russia, and the third secret was not revealed by the Vatican until 1960, at which time they said it had predicted the shooting of Pope John Paul II. When the appearance first occurred, the mayor threw the children into jail and threatened them with torture, even death in boiling oil for lying, but the children stuck to their story and were eventually released. The final appearance of the Virgin Mary occurred on October 13, 1917, and there were an estimated seventy thousand people who witnessed the famous Miracle of the Sun. The story goes that there was pouring rain and high winds on the morning of October 13, but at noon people all over the world testified that they saw the sky open up and the sun seemed to spin out of its axis and hurtle toward earth. Many thought it was the Judgment Day. However, only the three children saw the Virgin Mary that day. Two of the children subsequently died in the flu epidemic that swept Europe after the First World War. The third one, Lucia, became a Carmelite nun. She returned to *Fatíma* in 1967 for the fiftieth anniversary of the apparition when the pope was present."

"Wow! That's quite a story," said Dorothy.

"Yes, it is," agreed Katie, "and twice a year, on May 13 and October 13, pilgrims come from all around the world. There is often upwards of seventy-five thousand people in the town square all waving handkerchiefs as the Madonna passes through the crowd."

"Anyway, from *Fatíma*," continued Katie, "we return to Spain."

Agatha and Dorothy looked at each other, and Dorothy raised her eyebrows, thinking, no, I'm sure my nightmare won't come true. Jorha and Katie are the good guys, right?

"We'll be spending the night in Salamanca, Spain. This ancient city is famous for its university founded in the early twelve hundreds. At one time, Salamanca was on a par with Oxford, Paris, and Bologna as one of the four leading intellectual centers of the medieval world. It's still a university town. The city is built around the *Plaza Mayor*, which is an eighteenth-century Baroque Square considered to be the most beautiful public plaza in all of Spain, and that's saying something. I'm sure you will agree that we have seen some beautiful plazas. This square is not only beautiful but also contains a wonderful arcade of shops and cafes. Be sure to try the *Salamancan* drink of choice, *leche helada*, a refreshing vanilla and almond drink.** Most of the sights are within walking distance of the square. We'll be staying at the *Palacio de San Esteban*, a government parador which was converted from a former convent. I'll provide a map of the sites of interest and restaurants in the area so you can explore on your own."

"Assuming we are not all hauled in when we cross the border," whispered Dorothy to Agatha.

Agatha smiled at her and whispered, "I'm sure it will be fine. They are not supposed to bother us until we get back to Madrid."

"That's what they said," said Dorothy.

They all enjoyed their brief stay in *Fatíma*\*\*\* and found it interesting to see a woman of about forty years of age making her way across the square on her knees. A man, presumably her husband, walked beside her, and a couple of children periodically ran up to her, urging her on. In spite of all the support, the woman looked extremely uncomfortable, even with the pads she had on her knees, and her progress was very slow.

"Doing that is definitely not on my bucket list," commented Agatha to Dorothy.

"Mine either," agreed Dorothy.

After a short stay in *Fatíma*, they all climbed back on the bus for the trip to the Spanish border and, they hoped, beyond.

About three hours later, Jorha announced that they were entering Spain. No flashing lights were in sight and the bus went whizzing right across the border, and did not even have to stop.

"Well, that was easy," whispered Agatha to Dorothy.

"It sure was," Dorothy whispered back looking relieved. "Just like my dream, Jorha whizzed right through—just no blinking red lights trying to stop us. All that worrying for nothing! My subconscious was just being silly."

"It's only about another hour to Salamanca," said Katie to the group, looking up from her knitting.

The time went fast, and they were soon disembarking in front of the parador****.

"Wow! This is beautiful," commented Agatha as they walked through the entrance. "Another home run for Katie."

"It is," said Dorothy looking around.

After Agatha and Dorothy checked in, it was too early to call Jake to find out the latest, so they went up to their room to plan the rest of their day.

"This is really nice," said Dorothy as they entered their room.

"And it has a shower and a tub," said Agatha peeking into the bathroom. "I hope we'll have time for a nice soaking bath tonight. I need to be relaxed for what faces us tomorrow."

"I brought some bath bombs from home, but haven't had an opportunity to use them. I have enough for your bath, too," said Dorothy.

"Thanks," said Agatha. "That sounds heavenly."

"So, shall we just follow Katie's map for touring?" asked Dorothy.

"I guess so. Let's see, we start at the Roman bridge built in the year 89 B.C. Eighty-nine, imagine that," marveled Agatha. "Then to *Casa Lis*, also known as the *Museo de Art Nouveau*. A decorative art museum. You'll like that."

"Yup! I'm not very familiar with that museum. Our travel book says most of the artworks on display there were created between the late nineteenth century and the 1930s," read Dorothy.

"Let's see," said Agatha, "from there we walk by the University of Salamanca. The grand entrance is indeed pretty grand I guess. It dates from 1534 and is very intricate in its detail. It's called the doorway to heaven."

"I think there are a few people who would not agree that a doorway to a school is the doorway to heaven!" laughed Dorothy.

"True," responded Agatha. "Anyway, then we go to the *Catedral Nueva* or the New Cathedral. Hmm, new? It dates from 1513. Adjoining the New Cathedral is the *Catedral Vieja* or the Old Cathedral. That cathedral was started in 1140."

"Wow! Coming here makes you realize how young our country is," commented Dorothy, looking out the window at the beautiful city.

"Yes," agreed Agatha. "Our country is very young. Anyway, the main thing to see at the Old Cathedral is the altarpiece painted by Nicholas of Florence."

"Don't know him," said Dorothy.

"Well, we will soon meet him, or at least his work. From the cathedrals we see the *Casa de las Conchas,* or House of Shells," continued Agatha. "It's a restored 1483 house known for the four hundred simulated scallop shells on its facade. It's a monument to the Order of Santiago. Then we will be at the *Plaza Mayor*. Katie says it's the most beautiful public plaza in Spain. We shall see. At the plaza we can shop and have dinner. Are you game?"

"I'm game," responded Dorothy. "Let's go!"

Six hours later, they were back in their room, longing to soak their sore feet.

"Whew! That was great but I'm exhausted and my feet hurt," said Dorothy. "Let's take our baths. Do you want to go first?"

"No," responded Agatha, "that's all right. You go ahead. I'll put my poor feet up while you take your bath. Take your time. We can call Jake after both of us have bathed."

An hour and a half later, the ladies felt a lot better, though they were a little more wrinkly after their long soaks in the tub. Agatha dialed Jake.

"Good morning," answered Jake.

"Good evening, Jake," responded Agatha. "It's night here, not morning."

"I know," acknowledged Jake, "just kidding. It's morning here. How was your day?"

"Good!" said Agatha. "We're back in Spain. We were afraid the police would be waiting for us when we crossed the border, but they weren't. Dorothy even had a nightmare about it last night."

"No," laughed Jake. "The police are waiting until you get to Madrid."

"That's good," said Agatha.

"Does the group know what's going on yet," asked Jake.

"No," said Agatha. "I think Katie wanted them to enjoy the trip as much as possible before telling them."

"That's just as well," responded Jake. "We don't want anyone disappearing on us or having time to think up a good story."

"So true," agreed Agatha.

"By the way, I have some good news. The Madrid police have officially hired me as a consultant, so I have given them all the information I accumulated. Now I can research with their full support and on their dime. I've also gone over with them what we talked about at our meeting with Katie and Jorha the other day."

"That's wonderful," exclaimed Agatha. "I'm so glad you're going to get paid for all of your work."

"Yes, I'm grateful for the money, so thanks for getting me the job," said Jake, "but I've been happy to help you out, Agatha. I'll assist you anytime you need it. You know that don't you?"

"Yes, thank you. Its been really nice of you to help us, and I do appreciate it," blushed Agatha.

"All right, you two, back to business, if you please," interjected Dorothy.

"Okay," laughed Agatha. "Let's go over some of our facts. We know that several members of the tour have lied. Dan and Rick lied. They are a gay couple and live together in California. They didn't want the hassle of their fellow tour members knowing. Seems strange in this day and age, but whatever. The Zimmermans and Garcias lied. They're business people looking for areas to open yogurt shops and didn't want their competition to find out. They all seem to have a good excuse for lying."

"Yes, true" said Jake. "I've also found that they are not the only ones who have lied."

"Really!" said Dorothy. "Who else?"

"Stanley has lied."

"Stanley?" said Agatha. "You're kidding!"

"Not kidding. I checked with his college here in the States and as far as they know, he dropped out of school a year ago. They're not aware of his being in any study-abroad program."

"Hmm," sighed Agatha. "But he's so young to be a bad guy!"

"Agatha, remember about ten years ago—the Morrison case?" asked Jake.

"No... Wait. Yes, I do," said Agatha. "That was the case against a hit man. Right?"

"Yes," answered Jake, "and do you remember what he looked like?"

"Yes," said Agatha. "He looked very young, like a teenager. But, it turned out he was much older, about thirty."

"Thirty-two actually," said Jake.

"So you think Stanley is a hit man?" asked Agatha.

"What!" exclaimed Dorothy. "No way."

"No," said Jake, "I don't think Stanley is a hit man. I'm just saying that I think he's lying about being a student. From there, I don't know."

"Doesn't anyone tell the truth these days," commented Dorothy.

"So what's going to happen tomorrow?" asked Agatha.

"It's my understanding that the police will question Katie first, then Jorha. After them, they will want to talk to you and Dorothy."

"Us!" said Dorothy. "We don't know anything. Well, I guess we know more than most of them do. We at least met Robbie."

"The police will talk to everyone on the tour, and you two are the only ones who talked to him," said Jake.

"Us and Jessica," said Agatha.

"Yes, that's right, and Jessica," affirmed Jake. "She sat with him on the plane for a while, right?"

"Right!" said Agatha.

"The police will want to speak with everyone eventually," said Jake. "I have several other things to tell you."

"Really! What?" asked Agatha.

"I finally talked the police into digging up Rolf, and doing an autopsy," said Jake.

"Really?" squeaked Dorothy.

"Yes," responded Jake, "and toxicology already has a blood sample but no results as yet."

"That's wonderful," said Agatha. "Good work. The results will tell us something."

"What will the police ask us?" Dorothy asked. She was already feeling nervous. Dorothy had never been involved in anything like this before.

"The police will be interested in everything Robbie said to you and what his demeanor was like," said Jake.

"Frankly, he only talked nonsense," said Dorothy, "and his demeanor was that of a jerk! Sorry! I shouldn't be speaking ill of the dead."

"He was pretty obnoxious," agreed Agatha. "I don't think what we saw will be very helpful, and you have shared with them all of our thoughts, Jake, I'm sure."

"Yes, I have, but they will want to hear it all from you."

"It's a good thing I kept notes," said Agatha. "So is that everything, Jake?"

"Actually, no, not quite," said Jake. "It seems like everyone on the tour has been telling one lie or another."

"What!" exclaimed Agatha. "Did you find something about Dorothy and me?"

"No," chuckled Jake. "I found nothing on you two."

"What!" said Agatha even louder. "Have you been investigating us?"

"No, don't get excited," said Jake, "I was only kidding."

"Hmm! Who's left?" wondered Dorothy.

"Let's see," said Agatha. "There's the Johnsons, Katie, Jorha, Jessica, and the Dixons. I don't think we have found any of them in a lie."

"We have now," said Jake.

"On no," said Dorothy. "Who?"

"Well, I checked with AARP, and they did not pay for the trip for the Dixons. They have no contest like that."

"What!" exclaimed Agatha again. "Oh, no, not the Dixons."

"Actually, I thought you had some suspicions about Dave," said Jake.

"Yes, but not really serious ones," said Agatha, "and none about Diane."

"Also," continued Jake, "Jessica was in Spain, Morocco, and Portugal just three months ago."

"That's weird," said Agatha. "No wonder she's not that interested in touring. Was she on a tour last time?"

"No," answered Jake. "She was by herself."

"Was it before or after her parents were killed?" asked Agatha.

"Just before," answered Jake.

"Maybe she had good memories from her trip that she wanted to relive in trying to forget her parents' death," suggested Agatha.

"Yeah, maybe! But, that's not all," said Jake. "Wait until you hear this."

Jake proceeded to tell Agatha and Dorothy more things about several members of the tour that absolutely shocked them.

After the call Agatha thought about what Jake had told them. Is this information somehow what is behind these strange happenings, and if so, why? And which person is behind it all? Evil! There is evil somewhere out there, she thought. I can feel it. It feels just like when some of the really "bad guys" were in her courtroom.

# TRAVEL TIPS FROM AGATHA AND DOROTHY

"Murder on the Orient Express" is a well-known Agatha Christie novel where the murderer is actually multiple people.

** LECHE HELADA

Ingredients:

4 cups milk

1 cup sugar

1 cinnamon stick

The peel of one lemon

Ice cube

Cinnamon

Directions:

1. Place the milk in a glass bowl and heat in a microwave for 5 minutes on high.

2. Add sugar, cinnamon stick, and lemon peel. Cook another 5 minutes on high. Pour into another bowl and cool mixture.

3. Strain the mixture when cool and serve over ice. Garnish with cinnamon.

***Pilgrimages to Fátima take place on May 13 and October 13. If you plan on visiting around these days, you must make room reservations months in advance. Also, it is good to remember that this is a religious destination and is an early to rise and early to bed town. Not much night life, if that is what you are looking for.

****Palacio de San Esteban, is a government-rated five-star hotel, built in a former convent dating from the 1600s. Arroyo de Santa Domingo 3, 37001 Salamanca, tel. (92-326-22-96).

# CHAPTER 14

## Day 14

*Salamanca—Segovia—Madrid: As we return to Madrid, we will stop in the old town of Segovia, with its medieval buildings, unique Roman aqueduct, and the Alcázar standing three hundred feet above the valley. We will stroll around the twelfth-century walls and explore the narrow lanes of the Castile. We then return to Madrid, where this evening we enjoy a farewell dinner and toast "adios" to all our new friends.*

"Today will be a big day," said Agatha as she and Dorothy were waiting to board the bus.

"True," agreed Dorothy, "and we will find out if we get to leave for home, on schedule, tomorrow night."

"Not that I'm anxious to leave Europe," sighed Agatha.

"Yeah! It's been a great trip—if you disregard a murder or two," said Dorothy facetiously.

Katie took her place as the travelers settled into their seats, ready for their last day of touring. Katie planned to tell the group about the police situation after they left Segovia.

"Good morning," said Katie as cheerfully as she could manage. "We're returning to Madrid today, but first we'll stop in a town which typifies the glory of Old Castile, Segovia. You may want to keep your eyes glued to the windows because Segovia is located in the center of the most castle-rich part of Spain. This ancient city was retaken from the Moors in the eleventh century, and Isabella was proclaimed queen there in 1474. Queen Isabella, if you remember your history, financed Columbus. Segovia has a well-preserved, still-functioning Roman aqueduct that was constructed in the first century A.D. It also has many beautiful churches, mansions, and squares—all built against the backdrop of the Sierra de Guadarrama."

"How far is it to Segovia?" asked Ted.

"It's a little over one hundred miles," answered Katie. "It'll take us about two hours to drive there."

"Then how far is Madrid from Segovia?" Ted continued.

"Only about forty-two miles, maybe an hour's drive." said Katie. "We will be in Madrid by early afternoon."

"I wonder why Ted's asking?" whispered Dorothy to Agatha.

Agatha shrugged her shoulders.

The stop in Segovia was interesting. The aqueduct was amazing, and to think it was built so very long ago and was still functioning. It was made of mortarless granite with a hundred and eighteen arches, soaring to ninety-five feet at its highest point, and spanned the *Plaza del Azoguejo*, the old market square. The *Cabildo Catedral de Segovia*, built between 1515 and 1558, was majestic and beautiful, the group's last chance to marvel at the pinnacles, domes, and flying buttresses of Gothic architecture. Their last stop was the Alcázar, famous with Americans —especially Californians—because this castle was the model for the Sleeping Beauty Castle at Disneyland in Anaheim. Isabella first met her Ferdinand here, and the group peeked in at the facsimile of her bedroom. They also walked the battlements, from which boiling oil was poured on many an enemy below. A few of the hardy climbed the one hundred and forty-one hazardous steps to the tower, which originally was built as a prison by Isabella's father. Of course, the hardy included Agatha and Dorothy, who were not going to miss the view from the top.

The tour did not include the Esteban Vicente Contemporary Art Museum, and Dorothy realized they did not have enough time to run over on their own. Having been born in a small town just outside Segovia, Esteban Vicente lived in New York for most of his life and had a major role in developing American abstract art. Dorothy really wanted to go to this museum but would have to wait until their next visit to Spain (hopefully there will be one, thought Dorothy) to see the one hundred and forty-two works in the collection at the museum located in a newly renovated fifteenth-century palace. Darn!!!

Once the bus was headed to Madrid and Katie had given, as a reward, a large chocolate bar to each tour member who climbed the tower at the Alcázar. Katie knew now was time to tell the group about what they would face when they got to Madrid.

"Could I have your attention for one last time on our tour bus," started Katie as she stood and turned to the group in her familiar position, and then she paused and looked down. The expression on her face got everyone's attention.

"As you know," she finally continued, "some pretty horrible things have happened on this tour. I have never had anyone die on any of my tours, and we have had two deaths on this one. I am so sorry that these things have happened. You have all been real troupers."

"In spite of everything, the tour has been wonderful," said Rubio. "The deaths weren't your fault. The man on the airplane probably died of a heart attack or something, and Marian tripped and fell after she had too much to drink. Horrible occurrences, but life happens, even on vacation."

Everyone expressed agreement and support for Katie.

"Thank you so much," said Katie tearing up. "This group has really bonded. More than most groups. Probably because of the problems we have faced together."

"I agree," said Nancy. "We need to stay in touch through Facebook or something after the trip and share our pictures."

Again, everyone murmured their agreement.

Hmm, this wasn't going exactly the way Katie had expected. She had known it would be hard, but the group was making it even harder by being so nice.

"I have some things that I need to tell you," said Katie. "Things that you don't know as yet." Katie paused, looking down again. Looking back up at the group she continued, "Rubio said that Mr. Thomas probably died of a heart attack or something. Actually, once the body arrived back in the United States, an autopsy was performed. The authorities have recently found that Mr. Thomas did not die of natural causes."

The group was silent as they each processed that information.

Finally Stanley asked, "What does that mean?"

"It appears he may have been poisoned," explained Katie.

"You mean he was murdered?" asked Rick.

Someone in the group gasped. Agatha wasn't sure who it was. She turned to watch the group as they received the information. Would someone reveal themselves?

"I don't know," said Katie. "He may have taken something himself, I suppose."

"Weird place to commit suicide," commented Dan.

"Agreed, but the situation is that the police in Madrid want to talk to each of us when we get back to Madrid," said Katie.

"We're not going to be late going home, are we?" asked Ken. "I've got business deals pending when I get back."

"I thought you were retired," said Dave.

"I never said I was retired," retorted Ken. "I said that I live in a retirement community, but I'm not retired."

"I hope our departure will not be delayed," said Katie. "I'm not expecting it to be delayed at this time."

"Why are we being questioned?" asked Ted. "We may have been on the plane with this guy, but so were lots of other people. I personally never met the guy."

"Am I being questioned?" asked Stanley. "I wasn't even on the plane."

"As I understand it, everyone on the tour will be questioned," said Katie. "We are all being questioned because the police don't know whether or not some of the other weird things that have happened on this tour are connected to Mr. Thomas's death."

"You mean like Marian's accident?" asked Chelsie in a soft voice.

"Yes, Chelsie, like Marian's accident," said Katie. Ken's question about being delayed had been side-stepped, and he hadn't brought it up again. Thank goodness.

"How long have you known the guy on the plane was poisoned," asked Ted, "and why weren't we told sooner?"

"I really just found out," responded Katie. "It took a while to get the body back to the States, and then it took a while to do the autopsy and for the results to come back."

"That makes sense," said Linda.

"I'm so sorry the police feels it necessary to speak to everyone," said Katie. "Hopefully it won't be too unpleasant."

The remainder of the bus ride to Madrid was pretty quiet. Being interviewed by the police is something no one looked forward to. When the bus approached the hotel, two police cars could be seen parked in front. Agatha elbowed Dorothy, pointing to the cars. Dorothy glanced out the window and shuddered.

The group slowly emptied the bus and entered the lobby. Sophia was behind the desk and she smiled a welcome at the group as they filed in, then glanced over at a couple of men sitting in the lobby area. Everyone in the tour group was sadly aware that there was no little white dog barking a welcome. The two men, dressed in suits, stood as the group entered.

"Katie Matsen?" asked the taller of the two, looking over the group.

"Yes, I'm Katie Matsen," said Katie.

"I'm Detective Garcia," he said. "As I believe you have been told, I wish to speak with you and everyone on your tour. Please go ahead and get your group checked in, then we would like to talk to you, your driver, and to Agatha Johnson. Have the rest of your tour members wait in their rooms until we call for them. We'll wait for you here in the lobby."

"Okay," said Katie nervously, then walked up to the check-in desk.

"Hi," she said to Sophia. "Are our rooms ready?"

"They sure are," answered Sophia. "How was the trip?"

"In many ways, very good," said Katie, "and in other ways, not so good."

"Here are your room keys," said Sophia. "You have one less room on the return. Is that correct?"

"Hmm, unfortunately, that's correct," said Katie. "That's the 'not so good' part. Marian Locker fell in Granada and hit her head."

"Oh my goodness! That's too bad," commiserated Sophia. "Did she have to go home early?"

"Uh, no," said Katie. "Actually, she died of her injuries."

"Oh my gosh," said Sophia. "I'm so sorry. Someone on the tour died on the trip over too, right?"

"Yes," said Katie, lowering her voice, "It's horrible. That's why the police are here. I'll tell you more later."

"Okay," said Sophia, also speaking more softly. "You know the police came and dug up Rolf and took him away. They wouldn't tell us why. It has something to do with them being here today, doesn't it?"

"Yes," said Katie. "Rolf may have been poisoned when he drank the spilled drink."

"What! Oh my gosh," said Sophia shocked and barely managing to keep her voice down.

"Like I said," said Katie. "I'll talk to you later."

Katie handed out the room keys and asked members of the group to remain in their rooms, except for Agatha, who was to return to the lobby.

When Agatha stepped off the elevator in the lobby after getting her belongings settled in her room. She saw Jorha sitting with a uniformed police officer.

"Where's Katie?" Agatha asked as she walked over to Jorha.

"She's in with the police, being questioned," Jorha said nervously.

Agatha sat down next to Jorha on the couch and looked over at the policeman, who looked rather stern. She considered asking him some questions, but thought better of it. It was almost an hour before Katie emerged from a room off the lobby and told Jorha to go in.

"This is going to take a while," said Agatha to Katie. "You were in there a long time."

Before Katie could answer the policeman told them, in very good English, that they could not talk to each other until after Agatha had also talked to the detective.

I guess they didn't want Katie to tell me what she was asked and how she answered.

Seems reasonable, thought Agatha.

Agatha continued leafing through a magazine that had been laying on an end table, although it didn't really hold her attention. She had never been a witness or even questioned in a criminal case. Of course, she had seen lots of other people who had been in this situation in the courtroom. They were always nervous, and she could see why now. She was nervous too, even though she knew she wasn't guilty of anything. Why does being involved in something like this make you feel guilty?

Katie went to her room, with a warning not to talk to any of the other tour members until after they had been questioned.

About forty minutes later, Agatha was called in to speak to the detective. Detective Garcia told Agatha to have a seat, then returned to writing on the papers in front of him. He finally looked up and stared at Agatha for a minute, making her squirm uncomfortably.

"So you're Jake's girlfriend," he said.

That certainly surprised Agatha.

"Uh, no I'm not," she said. "I've known Jake professionally for many years, and we recently moved next door to him."

"Oh, from what Jake said, I guess I just assumed . . ," started Detective Garcia. "Never mind. I understand that you are the one who started to suspect something odd was going on during the trip."

"Yes, that's true," said Agatha. "Especially when I found that the rock embedded in my seat on the bus was actually a bullet. Then we started finding out that just about everyone on the tour was lying about something. Jake was . . ."

"Okay, okay, let's start from the beginning," interrupted Detective Garcia. "You are touring with a friend?"

"Yes, with my roommate, Dorothy Collins," answered Agatha. "We've been friends since childhood and decided to buy a house together to save on expenses so we could do a lot of traveling. Both of us have always wanted to travel but haven't had the opportunity. When we moved into our new home, we discovered that Jake Porter lived right next door. In fact, our walls are connected. Do you know Jake?"

Agatha paused, waiting for an answer and then realized she was rambling—giving a lot more information than was asked for, or wanted. She knew better from her court experience but she was nervous and that made her jabber on and on. Attorneys always told their clients to answer the questions directly and succinctly—to not give more information than is asked for. She had heard many attorneys advise their clients of this before court started. She didn't realize until now how difficult it was to follow that advice.

"Yes, I have met Jake," said Detective Garcia. "Did you have an opportunity to meet Robbie Thomas before he died?"

"Yes, he was on the shuttle bus that picked us up to take us to the airport," said Agatha.

"I hate to speak badly of the dead, but he was kind of an obnoxious fellow."

"Why did you think he was obnoxious?" asked the detective.

"Well, he was trying to hit on Dorothy," said Agatha.

"He hit Ms. Collins?" interrupted the detective.

"Oh no, no. I'm sorry, that's American slang," explained Agatha smiling in spite of herself. "Your English is so good, I didn't think. But colloquialisms are difficult, I know. I'll explain. Robbie wasn't actually hitting Dorothy, but he was flirting with her in an obnoxious way. He also kept interrupting the driver as the driver was telling us about the trip. We didn't like Robbie right off the bat—whoops, I did it again. We didn't like Robbie right away."

"Did you see him on the plane?"

"Yes."

"Did you talk to him?"

"Yes. When Dorothy and I went to the bathroom the first time, he was sitting with Jessica, and he introduced us to her."

"Jessica?"

"Yes, Jessica Whitley. She's a member of our tour."

"Did she sit with him the entire trip?"

"No. Later we noticed that she had moved her seat. You couldn't blame her. Like I said, he was pretty obnoxious."

"What was Robbie doing after she moved her seat?"

"I'm not sure. I think we heard him yell something during the movie but when we actually saw him again he was asleep, or, or, uh, maybe dead? I thought he was asleep at the time. He was drooling a little. We thought he looked disgusting! I feel so bad now. We should have checked on him. Maybe he was still alive. It never dawned on us . . . . ."

"Did you see anyone talking to him during the trip?"

"No. . . well, Katie probably talked to him. She stopped a couple of times to speak to each member of the tour, but I didn't actually see her or anyone else talking to him other than Jessica, and Dorothy and I, of course. After dinner and the movie, Dorothy and I both slept."

"Did you meet anyone else who was on the tour during the plane trip besides Robbie and Jessica?"

"Yes, we were sitting with Diane and Dave Dixon. We had center seats in the long row in the middle of the plane."

"Did they have any conversation with Robbie?"

"Not that I know of. I don't think they were aware of him. The tour members did not meet each other before the flight. Diane took a mild sleeping pill and slept more than Dorothy or me. Dave said he stayed awake though."

"How do you know he stayed awake?"

"Well," said Agatha, "I guess I don't know that for sure. He could have dozed while I was asleep. When I was awake he was usually reading."

"Did he ever leave his seat?"

"Not that I recall, but I'm sure he must have gone to the bathroom at least once. It was a long flight."

"Would he have walked by Robbie on the way to the bathroom?" asked the detective.

"Yes, if he went to the closest one."

"But, you didn't see Mr. Dixon have any contact with Robbie?"

"No. Of course anyone on the tour could have walked back and talked to him, or killed him for that matter, but I didn't see anyone else talking with him."

"When did you learn of Robbie's death?"

"On the bus. Katie reluctantly told us."

"Why do you say reluctantly?"

"Well, she was very late getting to the bus and wanted to leave right away to get to the hotel. I asked Katie what happened to Robbie Thomas, since I knew he was supposed to be on the tour with us. It was then that Katie told us that he had died on the flight. She had wanted to wait until the dinner that night to say anything."

The detective then switched to what had happened later that evening.

"You had a dinner with all of the tour members that first night?"

"Yes. A welcome reception, I think it was called."

"Did anything unusual happen?"

"Well, Diane spilled her drink, and the dog licked it up. Later, the dog died. Of course we didn't connect the dog incident to Robbie's death at the time."

"Who brought Diane her drink?"

"Just one of the waiters. We assumed her husband had sent it over, but later Dave said he hadn't."

"Did it look as though Diane spilled the drink accidentally?"

"Oh, yes. She was holding Rolf in her arms, and he tried to jump down. He made her spill the drink. Why would she do it on purpose?"

"Were you on the bus when the bullet went through the windshield?"

"No. Dorothy and I had stayed all day at the art museum. Dorothy was an art teacher before she retired and was thrilled to be at the Prado. We stayed until it closed, then went out to dinner. We didn't get back to the hotel until late that night, and Katie met us in the lobby and told us we could sleep in the next morning because the bus windshield had to be replaced."

"Who discovered that the so-called rock was actually a bullet?"

"Well, I did. It had embedded itself in my seat, and I dug it out with tweezers."

"Why did you dig it out?"

"Um, well, I was curious. You see, I've had rocks hit my car windshield before, and they never did that much damage, so I just wanted to see the rock. I was kind of embarrassed that I was digging around in the seat, and I stuck it quickly in my pocket when I got it out because Katie and Jorha were boarding the bus. I didn't discover it wasn't a rock until later that night. I think I was talking to Jake when I pulled it out of my pocket and found it was a bullet. That was a surprise. I marked many a bullet into evidence in my working career. I knew exactly what it was when I really looked at it."

"Jake tells me you were a court clerk for a judge."

"Yes, that's correct. In a criminal court. That's where I met Jake. He used to testify in cases all the time."

"Jake says you're very bright and that I should listen to you. None of this would probably have come to light but for your curiosity, and you asking Jake to investigate the backgrounds of the tour members. It led to the autopsy of Robbie—and the dog."

Agatha looked down at her lap and blushed. She never knew that Jake had such a high opinion of her.

"To continue," said the detective, "tell me about the night Marian Locker died."

"Well, we had another group dinner in Granada. We all had a lovely time. Lots of dancing and good food, and unfortunately, too much to drink for some in the group, especially Marian. Marian and Jessica were sitting at the table with Dan and Rick Rogers; the two younger unmarried women with the two younger unmarried men. Jessica left fairly early, as usual. She's still mourning, we think, over the death of her parents. They were killed in a car accident."

"Yes, that is what Jake told me."

"Anyway, the other three remained, and Marian apparently had a lot to drink. She even knocked some dishes on the floor when she stood up from the table, she was so unstable. The three decided to go for a walk, out in the fresh air. Dan and Rick said they left her at some point to go to bed, but she remained in the patio by the fountain. The kids found her body in the fountain when they came back from visiting the Gypsy caves."

"The kids?"

"Yes, Chelsie, Teddy, and Stanley, the youngest three on the tour. It was quite a shock for them. Chelsie saw the shawl that Diane had loaned Marian earlier in the evening floating in the water and went to rescue it. She found Marian looking up at her from beneath the shawl. At first she thought it was Diane but then realized it wasn't. So upsetting for her."

"Marian was wearing Diane's shawl?"

"Yes. Diane loaned it to her when the group decided to go for a walk because Marian had forgotten to bring a wrap and it was cool out."

"Did anything else happen that was unusual on the tour?"

"Well, we lost Katie and a camel in Morocco. I'm sure Katie told you about that."

"Yes, she did." Detective Garcia was silent a moment, thinking. "I can understand why you have been suspicious," he continued. "A lot of unusual things have happened on this tour. I can also understand why you were confused as to what was going on. So many disparate occurrences. There seems to be no connection between them. And no one target."

"Yes, it was all so strange. Then, Jake found out that almost everyone on the tour is lying about one thing or another," commented Agatha. "I have no idea what is going on; but now that we know Robbie and Rolf were poisoned, we do know something is up—uh—is wrong."

"Yes, and we do not have much time to figure it out. You all leave tomorrow, and I have no evidence to detain any of you. We'll get a few more tour members interviewed this afternoon and the rest in the morning, but I don't know that we will learn anything."

They both sat quietly thinking for a few minutes.

Finally Agatha said, "I have an idea."

Detective Garcia looked up skeptically.

"We know that Jake found a connection among some of the tour members," Agatha said, "a connection that most of the ones involved probably don't even know about. That could be at the crux of this matter."

"That is possible," said the detective, "but what is your idea?"

"What if we do what is done in many mystery novels. All of the tour members will be at the dinner tonight. What if I stand up and expose all of the lies and all of the connections among the tour members and see what happens."

"That could be dangerous," said the detective. "I don't think I can allow you to put yourself in that position. We may have a killer in the group somewhere. This is not fiction, this is real life. No, it's too dangerous."

"What's your alternative? To watch us all fly off tomorrow?" Agatha pressed. "Who knows, if the killer has not accomplished his or her goals on the trip, maybe he'll blow up the plane. I'd rather take my chances on the ground. Look, you could have your police as the waiters and be on the terrace where the dinner will be. I've been part of a criminal court staff for many, many years. It's not like I'm just some old lady off the street."

"You're hardly any old lady," the detective smiled briefly at Agatha. "But Jake would not be happy if I put you in danger."

"Maybe I'm in danger anyway. Look what happened to Marian. Was she killed? Chances are good that she was. And again, what's you alternative?"

"I don't really have one," said the detective reluctantly but obviously considering her plan. "All right! All right! I'll agree! But let's work out every detail before this evening. I don't want anything to go wrong."

That evening everyone was assembled for the dinner—the farewell dinner. Two weeks had gone so quickly. Agatha had been right when she thought at the beginning of the trip that by the end, all of these people would be her friends. They were her friends. She liked them all, but she was quite sure that at least one of them had a hidden evil streak. She wondered which one as she looked around the rooftop terrace. It was all so beautiful. The stars were out, and the city lights were twinkling all around them.

Dinner was excellent, as expected. The mood of the group was not as good as it should have been finishing up a successful tour. The tour had been fun, in spite of all that had happened. Tour members were in their party clothes, but they were all pretty quiet, not really in a party mood.

No one knew what Agatha was going to do, not even Katie. Only Agatha, Dorothy, and the waiters who were milling around the tables. Detective Garcia was in a small kitchen area, just off the terrace, at the ready if needed.

They had just finished dinner, and Agatha thought now was the time, before Katie stood up to give her farewell remarks and before anyone tried to leave. No one was going to be allowed to leave before Agatha had her say.

Agatha arose, heart pounding, and cleared her throat. "Could I have your attention please. I would like to thank Katie and Jorha for a wonderful trip."

"Here's to Katie and Jorha," said Rick as he raised his glass. Everyone joined in the toast.

"We all appreciate the work Katie has done and the good times we have had. But there's something else we need to talk about tonight. It isn't a pleasant topic, but we all want to go home tomorrow, and there is a chance that we won't we allowed to leave."

"What!" shouted Ken. "I'm leaving tomorrow. I have to be back home."

"And I hope you will be back," said Agatha, "but the police could keep us here. It's now known that there has been a murder. Robbie Thomas was poisoned."

"Who's Robbie Thomas?" asked Ken.

"He's the dude who died on the plane trip over here, I think," answered Rubio.

"Oh yeah," said Ken. "We didn't even know him."

"So we all say, but there is at least one person in the group who did know him," said Agatha.

"How do you know that?" asked Ted.

"I'll tell you a little later, but for now we have to figure out who killed Robbie, who tried to kill Diane..."

"What," gasped Diane. "What do you mean? Who would want to kill me? That's ridiculous!"

"An autopsy was done on Rolf, the little dog that was here at the hotel at the beginning of our trip. You remember," said Agatha noticing a few puzzled faces. "When it was learned that Robbie had been poisoned on the plane and autopsy was performed on Rolf. He was also poisoned, and with the same poison that killed Robbie. The poison was in the spilled drink intended for Diane."

"Well, it was probably her husband. Didn't he send the drink over to her?" said Rick.

"I did not," said Dave hotly. "Don't throw me under the bus!"

"It couldn't have been Dave," said Diane with tears in her eyes. "I don't like Sangria and Dave knows it. He knows I wouldn't have drunk it. But, there's no one who would want to kill me. That's so ridiculous."

Dave put his arm around his wife.

"Well, someone sent the drink over," said Agatha, "and the waiter who gave it to Diane can't remember who it was. Then, there was the windshield that had to be replaced."

"So," said Rick. "What's the big deal about that?"

"The big deal is that it wasn't a rock that broke the windshield, it was a bullet."

"A bullet," squealed Linda. "Our family was on the bus when it happened. All of us could have been killed."

"No one told us about a bullet," said Ted.

"Agatha, maybe that's enough," said Katie.

"No, it's not enough," said Agatha giving Katie a hard look. "This has to be completed. Everyone has a right to know what's going on, and we need to solve this mystery together or we can't go home."

Katie didn't say anything further, but she obviously didn't like it. She wanted her guests to go home happy, not disgruntled. Agatha is just making it worse she thought.

"The shot appeared to have been aimed at Katie," said Agatha. "I don't think anyone else was in danger on the bus. I would have been had I been in my seat."

"I need to leave," said Jessica getting up from her table. "I feel sick."

"NO!" said Agatha loudly, startling the group. "Everyone is staying until we are through," she said emphatically. "Everyone."

Jessica slowly sat back down. Diane moved her chair over next to Jessica's and put her arm around her. "It's okay," Diane crooned. "It's okay."

Tears had started running down Jessica's cheeks.

"I'm sorry," said Agatha, more softly, "but everyone has to hear this out. The only one who can leave is Teddy if he wants to, or if his parent's want him to."

"Heck no," said Teddy. "I'm staying."

There were a few chuckles at this, and the atmosphere lightened a little.

"I guess he can stay," said his dad.

"All right. To continue, the next incident was Marian's death," continued Agatha.

"But that was an accident," said Chelsie quickly, then added, "Wasn't it?"

"Maybe it was," answered Agatha, "but maybe it wasn't. Marian was wearing Diane's shawl. Did someone mistake Marian for Diane and hit her over the head, before she fell into the water and drowned? We don't know for sure, but it could have happened that way."

"But why would anyone want to kill me," asked Diane. "I'm just a normal housewife from small-town USA."

"I don't know," said Agatha. "You can't think of any reason?"

"No, of course not," said Diane emphatically.

"Now wait just a minute," started Dave, standing up and glaring at Agatha.

"Sit down, Dave," said Rick. "We want to go home tomorrow. Let's hear her out."

"Thanks, Rick," said Agatha. "Next, there was the crazy camel incident. Katie could have been killed on that occasion. It was just luck that a group came by and rescued her. It's been like the perils of Pauline on this trip, but to multiple 'Paulines'. Marian, Diane, Katie? Is there a target? Is it random? That's what makes it all so strange. There seems to be multiple targets or random targets."

The group was silent for a moment processing what they had heard.

Then Stanley said, "Are you saying that one of us is a murderer?"

Agatha let everyone think about that for a minute before she said, "Yes, I guess, that's what I'm saying."

"What makes you the detective?" growled Rubio.

"I'm not a detective, although I worked in the criminal court system for thirty-plus years, and I want to go home tomorrow. Does someone else want to take over and try to work this out?"

There were no takers. Agatha had been pretty sure there wouldn't be.

"Okay then," continued Agatha, "Now I think we better go over all the lies that have been told."

"Lies! What lies?" asked Ted.

"A lot of lies, have been told by members of this tour. Most of them are probably innocent and unimportant, but we need to explore all of them, to determine what is relevant and what isn't." Agatha looked meaningfully at the Zimmermans and Garcias.

Ken glanced at Rubio then said, "Well, it's true we haven't been exactly truthful, but it has nothing to do with murder."

"Yeah," said Rubio. "I'll confess, I don't really have relatives in Spain. Ken and I are looking to expand our yogurt business internationally, and that's why we didn't go touring with all of you many of the days. We were looking for sites for our new stores in Spain."

"Why lie about that?" asked Ted. "None of us would care that you were doing business on the trip."

"We didn't want to alert our competitors," said Ken. "We wanted to keep it a secret that we plan to go international."

"The police have checked, and the Zimmermans and Garcias do own frozen yogurt stores," confirmed Agatha.

"So, Rubio, are you related to Detective Garcia who was asking us all those questions today? I was thinking maybe you were since you had relatives all over Spain—or so we thought." said Stanley.

"No, he is not a relative," smiled Rubio. "Our having the same last name is just a coincidence."

"I don't see what yogurt stores have to do with someone trying to kill people on this tour," said Dave.

Agatha shrugged her shoulders and then looked at Rick and Dan. Rick had been looking down at his hands; but when the room went silent, he glanced up and met Agatha's eyes.

"Actually, Dan and I have not exactly been telling the truth either," said Rick. "Dan and I are kinda not brothers."

"How can you be kinda not brothers? Are you stepbrothers?" asked Linda.

"No, not exactly." Rick cleared his throat and then said, "Dan and I both live in LA, and we're domestic partners. Do you know what that is?"

"I don't," said Teddy.

"Hush," said Linda, placing a hand on Teddy's back.

"Well, I'm sure the rest of us know," said Ken, "but why lie about that in this day and age?"

"It just makes life easier when we travel," explained Dan. "No one thinks anything about it if we just say we're brothers. And it's no one's business."

"Marian was sure wasting her time going after you guys," said Stanley.

"Marian was a friend," said Rick indignantly. "I don't call making friends a waste of time."

"Maybe Marian found out about your secret, and one, or both of you, pushed her into the fountain," said Ted.

"We did not," Rick and Dan said simultaneously.

"It doesn't matter that much if people know about us," continued Rick. "We just prefer that people on a vacation not know so that it's not an issue. As Dan said, it's no one's business but ours."

"I don't see that any of this so far has anything to do with a murder," said Ted. "Are there anymore secrets?"

Agatha shifted her gaze to Stanley.

"Why are you looking at me?" asked Stanley. "I didn't lie about anything—well, not anything important."

"What did you lie about that was unimportant?" asked Linda.

Stanley looked down at his hands.

"He's not a student," said Chelsie. "Is that your point, Agatha?"

"I'm sort of not a student, right now," said Stanley looking up at Chelsie and then at the group. "My grandparents said they would pay for me to study abroad for a year. When they told me that I had just dropped out of school. I hadn't told my parents or my grandparents. They would have been angry if they had known I'd dropped out, but—but, I hated school and I was frustrated because I didn't know what I wanted to do with my life. I knew my grandparents wouldn't pay just to let me travel around Europe and get my head on straight, so I lied to them. It's true that this trip is my last hurrah before going home. It was just easier to continue the story I had been telling my family to all of you. Anyway, this year has been a success for me. I'm ready to go back to school. I know what I want to do with my life. I'm older and wiser than I was a year ago. Certainly wise enough not to be a serial killer of people I didn't know before this trip!"

Agatha didn't say anything but looked over at Diane and Dave. When Dave realized Agatha was looking at them, he exclaimed, "What! We didn't lie about anything. I thought you were our friend."

"This has nothing to do with friendship right now," returned Agatha. "I'm sorry, Diane, but the police checked with the AARP, and the organization said that they do not have any kind of contest where they give the winner a trip. They knew nothing about you or the tour."

Both Diane and Dave just stared at Agatha, perplexed.

"But," started Diane.

"Katie, how were you paid for the Dixons' trip?" interrupted Agatha.

"Uh, let's see," said Katie thoughtfully. "I received a letter on what looked like AARP letterhead. Then, I think the money was wired to our office. I wondered at the time why my tour company was chosen, but I didn't have time to follow up. I thought I would do it after the trip."

"I received a letter also," said Diane. "I just thought I was lucky. There was a telephone number, which I called, and spoke to a lady at AARP."

"Yes," said Katie, "I spoke to a lady also."

"That phone number belongs to a burner phone," said Agatha, "and, the so-called prize probably has something to do with the last really big revelation, which, I think, will come as a shock to most of you who are involved. Although, I have a feeling at least one of you knows about it."

Agatha allowed for a dramatic pause. Someone made a faint groaning noise, but Agatha wasn't sure who it was.

"Diane," said Agatha, "when we were on the bus leaving the airport our first day in Spain and Katie said that one of the tour members, Robbie Thomas, had died on the plane, I believe you said you knew someone in the past by that name. Is that right?"

"Yes, I knew someone named Robbie Thomas," said Diane with a disgusted look on her face. "That was a long time ago, and he's someone I do not want to be reminded of."

"I'm sorry, but you need to tell us how you knew him?" asked Agatha.

"I'd rather not," replied Diane. "It wasn't a very happy time in my life. The Robbie Thomas I knew was not a nice person."

"I don't think this one was either," said Dorothy, speaking for the first time.

"All right!" interrupted Dave. "What is this all about. Diane has put that period in her life behind her, and I don't want her upset about it again."

"I understand, Dave," said Agatha, soothingly. "But, we have to talk about it. I think it has something to do with our problem."

Diane began to cry softly.

"Diane, did you get the letter with the list of the tours members before the trip?" asked Agatha.

"Yes. I brought it with us," answered Diane.

"Did you notice Robbie's name on the list?"

"What? No. It wasn't on the list."

"Yes, it was. But, he was listed as Robert Thoma and not Robbie Thomas."

"That was my fault," said Katie. "I listed everyone by the name on their passports and leaving the "s" off Thomas was a typo that I didn't catch."

"Was it a typo?" asked Agatha. "Or, was it done on purpose?"

"No, it wasn't done on purpose," said Katie. "Why would I do that?"

"Maybe so Diane and Dave wouldn't know Robbie was going to be on the tour," said Agatha.

"Why—what—that doesn't make sense," stuttered Katie. "I'm confused. What are you talking about Agatha?"

"Diane, I'm afraid you are going to have to explain your relationship with Robbie," said Agatha.

"Okay-okay, if I must." Diane paused before continuing. " I went to high school with Robbie," said Diane, wiping her eyes. "He was four years older than me, and I was impressed when he asked me out on a date. I was a freshman and he was a senior. I went out with him one night, and, and—he raped me. They call it date rape these days. In those days, no one did anything about something like that. In fact, the other boys snickered about it. Thanks to Robbie it was all over school. It was awful."

Diane paused and looked at Dave.

"Do you need to know anything more?" asked Dave.

"Yes," said Agatha. "I'm sorry, but we need to know it all."

Diane looked around the group. Everyone felt her pain but was spellbound.

"Well, it turned out," continued Diane slowly, "I became pregnant. I was pregnant with twins."

"Did you raise the twins?" asked Agatha gently.

"No," gulped Diane, now sobbing. "I—I had to give them up for adoption. I was only fifteen years old, myself when I had them. I've thought of those little babies every day of my life. I keep track of their birthdays every year and wonder where they are and who they are."

Dave had his arms around her, and Diane hid her face in his chest.

"Diane," said Agatha gently. "Those twins are here."

"SHUT UP," yelled Jessica jumping up. "JUST SHUT UP YOU INTERFERING OLD WOMAN!"

Jessica had been standing and inching toward the exit, but Detective Garcia had come into the room and blocked her way. Jessica frantically looked around and then pulled a gun out of her purse. The police, dressed in their waiter costumes, had been moving slowing toward her but stopped when they saw the gun. Jessica kept backing up until her back was against the substantial iron railing surrounding the terrace.

"Stay back," Jessica said. "All of you stay back."

Jessica glared at Agatha with hatred in her eyes. "You old bag!" she yelled, "Why couldn't you mind your own business? I knew you were going to be trouble. I should have killed you a long time ago."

Jessica began crying again. Her hand holding the gun was shaking violently.

One of the policeman waiters stepped toward her.

"STAY BACK! Don't come any closer. I'll shoot. I will shoot. I have nothing to lose." Jessica's eyes darted around the room and landed on Diane. Dave pulled Diane closer to him.

"Robbie Thomas was just what I expected. He was bad! Very bad," sobbed Jessica. "He was dirty. DIRTY! When I identified him before we boarded the plane and spoke to him, he began hitting on me. Hitting on me, his daughter. He didn't know I was his daughter, but he knew he was old enough to be my Dad. He said we should share a room on the tour. Share a room? Share a room? No! So disgusting! He made me sick! I wanted to throw up. Share a room? He was bad. He deserved to die." Jessica began pacing back and forth, wildly waving the gun.

"I'm—I'm a chemist," she said, "and I work for a pharmaceutical firm. I knew what to put in his drink." A giggle escaped from deep within Jessica. "He was bad, so bad. Bad people deserve to die. He needed to die. I was successful. Everything went exactly as I planned.

It was so easy. I thought the rest would be easy." Jessica began to giggle hysterically, then suddenly stopped and looked again at Diane. "But you," she said a little more softly. "You weren't bad. You were kind to me. You confused me. I'm glad you didn't drink that poison. You're not bad. You're good. Oh, for a while, I thought you were pretending, trying to trick me, that you really were bad and just trying to cover it up. I hit you on the head with a large candle stick from the hotel lobby while you were looking at the fountain. You fell forward into the water, and I—I held your head under the water. But when I let go, I saw it wasn't you. It was Marian. Poor Marian! I didn't mean to kill Marian. She wasn't bad. You made me do that! That makes you bad? Doesn't it? But you were kind to me. I was so confused. I am so confused."

Jessica was crying again, tears and mascara streaming down her face.

"Why didn't you keep me?" Jessica begged looking at Diane again. "The people who adopted me were bad. They were evil. My so-called Dad—he abused me. My so-called Mother did nothing about it. She was weak. She was bad. She wouldn't help me. I was so unhappy my whole life. How is that fair? When I grew up, I searched and found out who my real parents were. Not those bad people. But I thought my real parents had to be bad too. They deserved to die. They gave me away. They gave me to those bad people. I had planned many ways I could kill you on this trip, and every way would look like an accident." Jessica giggled again. "I planned this trip. I was the lady you talked to supposedly at AARP. I killed my birth father. That was easy. I tried to kill my birth mother too, but it kept going wrong. Now I'm glad I didn't kill her. You are good. I finally figured it out. You're a victim, too, aren't you? Just like me." Jessica was looking at Diane intently.

Diane did not respond but looked at Jessica, horrified, her hand covering her mouth and her eyes wide.

"What about your twin?" asked Agatha calmly.

"My twin. Oh yes, my twin. My twin deserved to die too. I found out my twin was adopted by good parents and was having a happy life. How is that fair? I was miserable. You were happy and I hated you," Jessica said as she turned and pointed the gun at Katie.

Katie gasped. "You're my sister?" she breathed.

Katie looked at Diane. "And, and—you're my birth mother?"

No one moved or said a word.

Suddenly, Jessica yelled, "I'M SORRY! I'M SO SORRY! I AM THE ONE WHO IS BAD!" Jessica quickly put the gun to her forehead and, before anyone could reach her, pulled the trigger. The thrust of the bullet propelled her backwards, over the iron railing, and she fell ten stories to the street below.

# CHAPTER 15

## *Day 15*

---

*Madrid—Los Angeles: Hasta la vista as we wing our
way home with wonderful memories of the beautiful
countries we visited.*

---

A gatha and Dorothy were up by eight, even though they did not get to bed until after two. They knew they had a long flight ahead of them, on which they could sleep later, and they needed to finish packing. When Agatha came out of the bathroom, Dorothy was sitting by the window just staring into space.

"Are you okay?" asked Agatha.

"I guess," said Dorothy. "I've never known a murderer before, and I've certainly never seen anyone kill themselves. It's very upsetting. I know you're experienced in these sort of things."

"What!" exclaimed Agatha. "It's true, I have seen murderers before, but I didn't really know them, and I've never seen anyone kill themselves either. On top of it all, I feel kind of responsible." Agatha sat down on the bed.

"Oh, Agatha! I'm so sorry," said Dorothy going over and putting her arm around her. "You mustn't feel responsible for Jessica committing suicide. You didn't hold a gun to her head. I think Jessica was a very sick person. The truth had to come out or someone else may have been killed. You did the right thing."

"I know that intellectually, but I just feel so bad that Jessica had to die. Maybe she could have been helped."

"I don't know. She said she thought her adopted parents were bad, too. I wonder if she was responsible for their deaths," said Dorothy.

"I wondered the same thing," said Agatha, "but Jake said there had been a thorough investigation after the accident, and they couldn't prove anything against Jessica or anyone else. The life insurance company was suspicious but finally paid up. I guess no one will ever know for sure if she killed them. Her parents were worth a great deal of money, and there was also a lot of life insurance, Jake said."

"I wonder who gets it all now?" thought Dorothy out loud.

"Well, it'll go by the terms of Jessica's will, if she has one, or, if she doesn't, to her next of kin."

"Wow! That's Diane and Katie isn't it?"

"No, I don't think so. All those relationships are severed with a legal adoption," explained Agatha. "Her next of kin would be in the adopted family."

"That's too bad for Katie and Diane," said Dorothy. "Maybe there are cousins or something who will get the fortune."

"Maybe," agreed Agatha.

Just then the phone rang, making them both jump.

"Hello," said Agatha reaching across Dorothy to answer it. After a pause, she said, "Sure, come on down. See you in a minute."

"Who was that?" asked Dorothy as Agatha hung up the phone.

"Katie," answered Agatha. "She and Diane are going to come down to our room. She said she has some things to talk to us about. I hope they're not too upset with me."

Five minutes later there was a light tap on the door.

"I'll get it," said Dorothy.

"Come on in," exclaimed Dorothy as she pulled open the door.

Both Katie and Diane looked pretty disheveled, and their eyes were red from lack of sleep and probably from crying. They had at least changed out of their party clothes and were both wearing sweat suits.

They hugged Dorothy and then Agatha, before sitting down on the edge of the nearest bed.

"Have you had any sleep?" asked Agatha.

"No, we haven't been to bed yet," said Katie. "But I wanted to see you two before we collapsed. Jorha's going to take care of getting everyone to the airport this afternoon, and I wanted to be sure to thank you for all you did. You were such a support on the trip, with everything that was going on, and last night—last night. . ."

"Last night did not turn out the way I wanted it to," said Agatha softly. "I'm glad you're not upset with me and I'm glad the truth came out, but I'm so very sorry about Jessica."

"You can't blame yourself," said Diane. "You had no way of knowing she would do something like that."

"I know. That's what Dorothy said," responded Agatha. "But I'm still appalled at myself for not foreseeing it and thinking of something that would have stopped her."

"I don't think anyone could have stopped her, and maybe it was for the best," said Katie. "She was a very unhappy person and mentally unbalanced. I wonder what her Dad did to her? I knew I was adopted, but I wasn't unhappy. I have good parents. I didn't know that I had a twin. I would have liked to have known that."

Diane put her hand over Katie's.

"How much did you know, before you went into the dinner last night?" Katie asked Agatha. "Did you know Jessica was the culprit?"

"No,—no I didn't know everything. Jake found out that Robbie, Diane, and Dave were all from Troy, Ohio and were about the same age. It wasn't until the night before the dinner that Jake learned that Diane had twins when she was very young and that Robbie was the father. Then, right before the dinner, Jake called and told me he had traced the twins, and that they were you and Jessica. So I figured one of the four, or some combination thereof, was trying to kill the others. I had no idea who or why. I was hoping that reveling everything would cause the guilty party to react. I'm so sorry Diane. I know it was very hard on you, and I'm so sorry about Jessica."

"I felt drawn to Jessica," said Diane as tears began to well again in her eyes. "Instinct I guess, a mother's instinct."

"But good did come out of it," said Katie. "We found each other."

"That's true," said Diane, "and I'll never let you go again."

Mother and daughter hugged each other. As Agatha watched, she could see the resemblance. And when you really thought about it, there was a mild resemblance with Jessica too, although she had dark coloring and took more after Robbie. Robbie had probably been pretty good-looking when he was young. Robbie wasn't a very good person. Does someone inherit 'badness'? Jessica thought everyone around her was bad. But she was bad too. Did that come from Robbie or because of her adopted family?

"We're both staying in Spain until the body is released so we can take it back to the States for burial," informed Katie.

"That's nice of you," said Dorothy.

"Well, it's the least we can do. She was an only child, and I don't know if there is anyone else to be there for her," said Diane. "Also, they found a handwritten will in Jessica's room. We haven't seen it yet, but Detective Garcia told us that it leaves most of her estate to Katie and me. I don't know if it is valid, being handwritten, and it probably had no witnesses. I don't know how that all works."

"Oh, my goodness!" exclaimed Dorothy.

"I'm so happy for you," said Agatha. "Yes, a handwritten will is good and does not have to be witnessed under California law, and she was a resident of California. It's called a holographic will. Jake told us that Jessica inherited a great deal of money from her parents. You are both going to be very well off."

"We really don't know too much at this time," said Katie, "but I want you to know that the cost of your trip is going to be refunded. I'm going to refund everyone's money that was on the tour. And, if we do inherit assets, there will be a bonus for both of you. If it weren't for you, I think that either Diane or I would be dead, and, perhaps, both of us. Thank you is not nearly enough but thank you again, so much."

"Yes, thank you," joined in Diane. "I feel guilty though, taking that poor girl's money. It was my fault that she went through what she did."

"Listen," said Agatha, "you've been through so much these past couple of weeks, on this trip as well as what you went through twenty-eight years ago. You are not responsible for the bad actions of others. You wanted the best for your children, and you knew you couldn't give it to them at that time. What you did was noble and difficult. Jessica wanted you to have her estate. You gave her comfort in her last days. I think you were healing to her, and she finally realized what she had done and what she almost did. She found that you and Katie were good people, and I think she began to love you in her own way. Love is healing. Goodness is healing, and you and Katie are good."

"They also found a notebook in Jessica's room," said Katie. "The police said it had many different ways to kill someone so that it would look like an accident. Isn't that awful? Included was the gunshot through the bus window, a list of poisons that are hard to detect—ha, even the runaway camel idea with the name of that Arab who would help her. There were many more ways that weren't used—yet! Had she gotten on the plane would she have poisoned me? I don't know.

I think Diane would have been safe. It's just all so sick. I can't believe she was my sister."

Tears flowed freely for some time, but finally Katie said she had to get to bed or she would keel right over, and Diane agreed. They all knew how to get in touch with one another after they returned home, and so they said their good-byes.

As the door closed behind them, Dorothy looked at Agatha and said, "Do you know what that means?"

"What, what means?" asked Agatha.

"That we are getting all our money back from this trip," answered Dorothy.

"What does it mean, other than it will be nice to have the money back?" asked Agatha.

"It means," said Dorothy, with a big smile, "that we do not have to start saving for our next trip. We can start planning it as soon as we get home."

# CHAPTER 16

Agatha and Dorothy had been home for more than a week when they had their first opportunity to get together with Jake. At least now they were over their jet lag.

Jake had been out of town at a conference when they returned, so they hadn't seen him as yet. Even though Agatha had talked by phone with Diane and Katie twice, it was all beginning to seem like a dream. However, Dorothy was still having an occasional nightmare about that last evening in Madrid. No doubt many of the others on the tour were having similar nightmares, especially the young ones. So sad!

Jake had invited them over tonight for that steak dinner he had promised. The one they had taken the raincheck on before they had left for the trip. The girls were bringing a big pitcher of ice-cold La La Lemonade herb tea* and dessert.

Agatha and Dorothy knocked on Jake's door promptly at six-thirty.

"Come on in," Jake yelled, "I'm in the kitchen."

"Hi," said Jake as the girls walked in.

"Hi," they responded. "It smells good in here."

Jake gave them both a big kiss on the cheek, perhaps lingering a little longer on the one he gave Agatha.

"I hope you're hungry. What you smell is my special garlic parmesan potatoes au gratin."**

"Yum!" said Agatha. "Sounds great. We are starved."

"I'm so glad you two are home safe and sound. I want to hear everything about your trip," said Jake, "but let's wait until your fabulous dessert before we talk about Jessica. I don't want to spoil our appetites. Does that work for you?"

"You bet," said Agatha. "We have lots to tell you even without the bad part of the trip. Spain, Morocco, and Portugal were so beautiful and interesting."

"I hope you brought plenty of pictures," said Jake.

"Yup," said Dorothy. "Lots of pictures."

"And we have Dorothy's sketches also," added Agatha. "And my written journal. Are you sure you're up for all of this?"

"Sounds good," laughed Jake. "I'm up for it. We have all evening. I thought we would eat outside, so come on out back while I grill the steaks. How do you like yours?"

"Both medium, please," responded Dorothy.

"This is nice out here," said Agatha, stepping out on the patio and looking around. "Dotty, we'll have to get some patio furniture. Now that we're home, we may want to sit out on our patio. Maybe get a barbecue too."

"Definitely," agreed Dorothy, sitting down. "These chairs are very comfortable. Where did you get them?"

"I actually ordered them online," said Jake. "I'll give you the website if you like."

"Please, we'll take a look," said Agatha.

"Okay, the steaks are on. Let's look at those pictures," Jake said as he sat down next to Agatha and picked up her laptop and started looking through the pictures. "Hey, that's a great picture of Dorothy in front of the Prado. One of the world's great art museums."

"I was so thrilled to be there," sighed Dorothy. "It was a dream come true."

An hour and a half later, the delicious meal had been consumed. They had looked at all of the pictures, Dorothy's sketches, Agatha's journal, and the girls had told their stories.

"Wow," exclaimed Jake, "I almost feel like I went on the trip too. You were right, those countries are so beautiful and interesting. It looks like you had a great time, except for Jessica and her activities, of course."

"We did. Next time we go traveling, you should come, too," said Agatha smiling.

"Hmm, maybe," laughed Jake. "But I've traveled a lot in the past and now I'm kind of enjoying staying at home for a while. I'm sure I'll get the bug to travel again."

"Well, we shall see if we can entice you sometime. Are you ready for dessert," asked Agatha, "or do you want to wait awhile?"

"I'm too full," said Dorothy patting her stomach.

"I'm kind of full, too," agreed Jake. "Why don't you tell me about Jessica and that whole aspect of the trip, then we can have dessert afterwards to sweeten our mood."

"Okay," said Agatha. "Where do we start? Jessica was a pretty little thing but always looked very sad and didn't really associate much with anyone on the tour."

"Yeah, we all felt sorry for her," added Dorothy. "She often didn't go on the day outings. We all tried to make friends with her and make her feel included, but she rejected most of our efforts. Diane was the only one who seemed to make any progress with her."

"After you told us about her parents' death, we felt even more sorry for her, never dreaming that she was actually dangerous and, well—wicked," said Agatha. "Apparently, Jessica had planned many ways that she could kill Robbie, Diane, and Katie on the trip and have it look like an accident. When one didn't work, she went on to the next method. She was very patient and clever. The poison she used on

Robbie, and tried to use on Diane, as you know, is difficult to detect, and unless foul play is suspected, would probably not be found. Had the bullet hit Katie, chances are it would have been thought to have been a random shooting, which does happen occasionally in big cities. Marian's murder was the most violent, but that too was thought to have been an accident at first—a tragic trip and fall by someone very intoxicated. There was no evidence connecting Jessica to Marian's death because she had no connection of any kind with her."

"Jessica must have been shocked when she heard that she had killed Marian instead of her target, Diane," commented Dorothy.

"I'm sure she was, but it was not enough to stop her. She apparently was not concerned about collateral damage because she continued to try to kill her birth family. After Marian was killed, we then had the camel incident," said Agatha, "when Katie and the camel disappeared in Morocco."

"The police found that Jessica had paid someone to separate the camel from the line of tourists and drive it into the desert," said Jake. "He was arrested."

"Katie could easily have died in the heat. Her phone wouldn't work, she had very little water, and she had no idea which way led back to the town. Thank goodness that group of Brits came by," said Dorothy.

"Yes, it was a close call for her," added Agatha. "But, then all the weird stuff stopped. I guess that was when Jessica finally realized that Katie and Diane were not evil people," said Agatha. "It must have been a difficult transition in thinking for her."

"So I guess she was hoping to just go home, with no one figuring out what had been going on," said Jake.

"I think so, but she realized there could be a problem once the police got involved," said Agatha. Agatha took a sip of lemonade herb tea as they all imagined what Jessica must have been thinking.

"There was a clue that we missed," said Agatha. "I've been thinking about it. We were at dinner one night in Portugal and we thought we heard Katie talking in the booth behind us, but when we looked we discovered it was Jessica. The two actually sounded a lot alike. It never dawned on us that they were related, and I never thought to mention it to anyone"

"It's interesting she left a will," said Dorothy. "It appears she wrote it after she learned that the police were getting involved."

"A will and some other ramblings," said Agatha.

"Did she write about the murders?" asked Jake.

"Oh yes," answered Agatha. "The night before her death she wrote that she had wondered her whole life about who her parents were. She said she hated these 'real' parents more every year. Once she was grown up, she hired someone to help her find out who her parents were, and she also discovered she had a twin sister, a twin sister who had a good life, with, apparently, good parents. She thought that was so unfair, so she hated her sister too."

"I was told by investigators that she had files full of information about Robbie, Diane, and Katie in her home," added Jake.

"She was fixated," said Dorothy. "That fixation must have become more and more bizarre over time."

"Such a waste," said Agatha. "She was so beautiful and, also, very smart. She could have had a wonderful relationship with Diane and Katie after finding them. Instead Jessica went to Spain, Morocco, and Portugal last year, tracking where the tour would go, and made her plans on the various ways she could kill the three of them. Then she made sure all three of them were on the tour. She came up with the idea of Diane and Robbie winning the trip so she could pay the expenses and be sure they would go. Neither could have afforded the trip otherwise. Jessica must have been feeling pretty confident when Robbie's death went so easily."

"Did she say anything about her adoptive parents?" asked Jake.

"No. Nothing," replied Agatha.

"I spoke to the officer who investigated the parents' accident, and he said that he looked at the case again but saw nothing that would encourage him to reopen it. So, unless Jessica left something confessing to their murder, I guess that matter is closed also," said Jake. "If she did kill her adopted parents, she did it in such a way that it was not detectable."

"My namesake, Agatha Christie, once said that murder is simple if no one knows it's a murder. That's true. I'm sure many murders go undetected, and that certainly was Jessicas's plan for Robbie, Diane, and Katie. Obviously Jessica was capable of killing her adoptive parents. Who knows whether she did or not, but I'm actually glad that they can't pin their deaths on her," said Agatha. "If it was proven that Jessica had killed her parents she would lose her inheritance from them per the California Probate Code. A murderer can't profit from his or her crime. As it is, Jessica was a very rich girl, and Jessica's will left one-third of her estate to Diane, one-third to Katie, and one-third to an organization that helps abused children. Katie believes Jessica's estate is about fifty million dollars, after taxes. Amazing, huh?"

"Whew!" said Jake. "That will be one big change in the lives of Katie and Diane."

"Dave, too," said Dorothy. "Not to mention their children. It's like winning the lottery. Perhaps they will find some happiness with the money. I hope so anyway. They are all good people and apparently were living happy lives before this happened. Katie and Diane now have each other, and hopefully the money will make their lives better and not worse. Lottery winners don't seem to fare well from what I read."

"Let's hope they will be happy," agreed Agatha. "But, Jake, you haven't heard the best part yet."

"Wait 'till you hear, this" smiled Dorothy.

"What?" asked Jake leaning forward across the table.

"Well, you know Katie refunded everyone's money for the tour," said Agatha.

"Actually, no, I didn't know that," said Jake. "That was very nice."

"Everyone on the tour was pretty traumatized," said Dorothy. "I think it was warranted, and she can afford to do it now with her inheritance."

"But what's even better than that," continued Agatha, "is that Diane and Katie are going to give us a bonus when they get their money. Isn't that great? They haven't told us the amount yet, but Katie said it would be six figures."

"Wow," exclaimed Jake. "Six figures! Your travel future is secure."

"I know," agreed Agatha. "Isn't that wonderful?"

"We will have the money to go wherever we want to go," said Dorothy enthusiastically, "And in the style in which we want to go," added Agatha.

"I'm happy for you," said Jake. "You deserve it. Jessica's evil plans might have been successful but for you."

"I'm glad we could help," said Agatha.

"Actually, I didn't do much," said Dorothy.

"I probably wouldn't have done what I did if you weren't there for moral support," said Agatha. "And both you and Jake were there to bounce ideas off of. Oh, and by the way, Jake, Katie and Diane are not forgetting about you. When we told them how you had helped, they were very grateful, so you will get a bonus also."

"That isn't necessary," said Jake. "I ended up getting paid as a consultant for my investigation by the Spanish police force."

"You can take the bonus, can't you," asked Agatha. "There's no prohibition is there?"

"No, not really," said Jake. "Not any more. If I was still working for the Santa Ana police, I wouldn't be able to take it. But I am self-employed now as a consultant, so I can take a fee from anyone. I have never received a bonus before. I like the idea. Adding a little padding to my retirement savings would be nice. But it really isn't necessary."

"Well, you deserve it. Katie and Diane said they are planning to deliver the checks in person so they can meet and thank you," said Agatha.

"I'll look forward to it," said Jake. "Say, it's getting a little cool out here. How about we go inside and dig into that chocolate creation you brought for desert. What is it?"

"It's actually a clue to where we are going next fall on trip number two," said Agatha scooting back her chair.

"Really!" said Jake.

"Yes," said Dorothy. "They're called chocolate-filled Russian tea cakes."***

Jake sighed as he followed the girls inside, thinking of all the trouble the girls could get into in Russia.

# TRAVEL TIPS FROM AGATHA AND DOROTHY

*La La Lemonade is made from dried lemon peels, rosehips, apples, and strawberries. Great hot or cold.

**GARLIC PARMESAN POTATOES AU GRATIN

Ingredients:

3 cloves garlic

2 lbs. white potatoes thinly sliced

Salt and pepper to taste

1 tablespoon butter, soft

1/2 cup heavy cream

Finely grated parmesan cheese

Whole milk

Directions:

1. Preheat oven to 350 degrees. Rub the butter all over the inside of a 12-by 8-inch baking tray or roasting pan and set aside.

2. Slice potatoes as thin as possible; use a mandolin if available

3. Heat the cream, milk, and garlic in a pot until it starts to boil and starts to thicken slightly. Take off the heat.

4. Place one layer of the potato slices in even rows and slightly shingled on the bottom of the baking dish.

5. Season with salt and pepper and cover with lots of parmesan.

6. Place another layer of potatoes on top of the first layer going in the opposite direction and season again. Sprinkle more cheese on top.

7. Repeat with a final layer of potatoes ending with a cheese layer on top. Season again.

8. Slowly pour the hot milk mixture over the layered potatoes making sure to cover all of them and place in the oven. Bake for about 45-50 minutes or until the tip of a sharp knife can go through the potatoes.

### ***CHOCOLATE-FILLED RUSSIAN TEA CAKES

Ingredients:

1 cup butter, softened

1/2 cup powdered sugar

1 teaspoon vanilla

2 cups flour

1/4 teaspoon salt

3/4 cup pecans, finely chopped

48 milk chocolate stars

1 cup powdered sugar

1 tablespoon red sugar crystals

Directions:

1. Heat oven to 400 degrees.

2. In a large bowl, beat butter, powdered sugar, and the vanilla until well blended.

3. On low speed, beat in flour, salt, and pecans.

4. For each cookie, shape a scant tablespoon of dough around one chocolate star to make a one-inch ball.

5. Place two inches apart on an ungreased cookie sheet.

6. Bake 12 to 15 minutes or until set and the bottoms start to turn golden brown.

7. To make the coating combine powdered sugar and red sugar, and mix well.

8. Immediately remove baked cakes from cookie sheets and roll in sugar coating.

9. Cool completely on cooling racks, about 30 minutes.

10. Roll in sugar coating once more.

Agatha likes to pile these on a plate and drizzle chocolate over them. She serves them, of course, with herb tea.

Agatha and Dorothy's next adventure...
# DEATHLY CRUISE
*to the* **BALTIC SEA**

Donna and Phil touring Madrid.

Donna Bashaw lives with her husband of fifty-seven years in Henderson, Nevada. She is the mother of three, the grandmother of eight, and the great-grandmother of six and counting. After teaching music for twenty-five years and then practicing law for twenty-five years, she is blissfully retired. She now spends her time traveling, ballroom dancing, writing, and doing various musical activities. Visit her website at donnabashaw.com.